RED

D1284258

Solara Gordon

EROTIC ROMANCE

Siren Publishing, Inc.
www.SirenPublishing.com

A SIREN PUBLISHING BOOK
IMPRINT: Erotic Romance

RED HOT
Copyright © 2010 by Solara Gordon

ISBN-10: 1-60601-799-3
ISBN-13: 978-1-60601-799-9

First E-book Publication: September 2010

Cover design by Jinger Heaston
All cover art and logo copyright © 2010 by Siren Publishing, Inc.

Printed in the U.S.A.

PUBLISHER
Siren Publishing, Inc.
www.SirenPublishing.com

DEDICATION

Thank you to the following:

To Laurell K. Hamilton, for inspiration and sharing her journey along with her wonderful books; to R.H.R. (RIP), you lit the fire of curiosity many years ago and exposed me to wonderful world of wondering and bringing to life, via the written word, the dreams that ensued; to family and friends (blood and non-blood alike) for your encouragement and support; to Mary Alice Pritchard, for your patience and encouragement during revisions and edits; and to Jim (DABear), for being there through it all and loving me as much as you do. Finally to my critique partners (the mud puddle), thank you for sharing this journey with me. This one's for you! Here's to many more to come!

Solara

RED HOT

SOLARA GORDON
Copyright © 2010

Chapter One

"Here's to you." With his raised coffee cup, Tom Haney, Assistant Station Commander, saluted Brent Stephens, Jameston, Virginia's Fire Chief and Lead Emergency Medical Technician. Their weekly lunch meeting had turned into an impromptu celebration of Brent's first three months full time on the job.

"Thanks. Sometimes it's hard to believe that six months ago I began the move to here from New York. Change can be good. I'm glad I decided to go through with it." Brent pushed his plate away and picked up his cup.

He grimaced as he sipped his coffee. Sweet coldness filled his mouth. No matter what others said about iced coffee, he liked his hot, black, and sweet. Right now, he needed the caffeine. Six hours of paperwork and packing the retiring chief's remnants of files took more mental energy than he realized. Duty rosters and reports awaited him when he got back to the station. He drank a few more swallows before setting the cup aside.

"Sorry the meeting took longer than expected." Tom pointed toward the front of Kater's dining room. "I'll get Bunny's attention next time she passes and get us refills."

Brent nodded. Normally, two to three people served the lunchtime crowd. Today marked the first day of fall. Most of the tourists and seasonal help were gone. Bunny worked the counter and dining area by herself. She'd grabbed his attention at their first introduction ten months prior. Even now, as then, his spark of interest had grown with each interaction. He wondered if her curiosity about him matched his about her.

Bunny Kater passed their booth, coffee pot in hand, her firm backside drawing quite a few admiring stares as she leaned forward to refill a patron's cup near them. "One fine set of cheeks, if you ask me." Tom's voice boomed as he turned around. Every patron in Kater's Café stopped eating and looked at Tom or Bunny. Brent wished Tom had lowered his voice before he spoke.

"More coffee, Chief?" a southern-accented feminine voice purred.

Bunny's shoulder-length brunette hair framed her heart-shaped face. Her hair, hazel eyes, and plump, pink lips set Brent's internal smoke detector off. She stood five feet seven in heels with legs that drove a man to fantasizing. She'd probably fit nestled up against him short of eye level in bare feet.

Bunny's petite waist and feminine curves masked her underlying strength and character. Her keen business acumen and well-known reputation for keeping her word preceded her throughout Jameston. She jogged with two of his staff and attended the local firemen's exercise class.

Watching her bench press her weight and topple his heaviest fireman in his recent self-defense class, Brent understood not judging a book by its cover. The woman's gym clothes raised more than his eyebrows. His tented uniform pants gave new meaning to rising to the occasion.

Tom's foot connected with his. Brent moved his shin, rubbing it with his other foot. He'd better get his libido under control. Brent shifted, sliding his cup forward.

Bunny stood two feet from him. Perky breasts filled out the shirt-covered space between her apron and nameplate. If he turned his head just right...

"Sure, Bunny. How about some apple crisp to go with it?" His stomach groaned, protesting the idea of more food. Brent watched Bunny wiggle away. Damn, he was getting as bad as Tom. The woman did fill out a pair of shorts nicely.

* * * *

Bunny smiled. She resisted looking back and winking at Brent. Something about a man in uniform connected deep in her psyche, drove her hormones into overdrive, and raised her internal temperature ten degrees. Not just any uniform, though. No, only firefighters sent her lust into a raging inferno.

She liked them tall and lean. Brent fit the description almost perfectly. His long legs and arms fascinated her and had her id conjuring midnight dreams she dared not discuss outside the bedroom. Short light-brown hair and dark brown eyes complemented his well-toned, muscular build, chiseled jaw, and Romanesque nose. She kept her eyes and mind off his large hands and feet. Otherwise, she'd be centered on his crotch, wondering if the folktale rang true.

Muscles, tight pecs, and washboard abs, along with a firm ass filling out a crisp, tailored uniform, dispatched hot flames of wanton need straight between her legs. Since her last break-up, sex hadn't mattered. Well, coupled sex hadn't. She'd worn out two vibrators.

Her best friend, Amy, swore getting laid might help cool things down. Bunny wasn't sure she wanted cooling down. The heat level of her fantasies felt good on a lonely night. Getting next to someone didn't carry the thrills it once had.

Amy kept dropping hints about setting Bunny up. Blind dates gave her the heebie-jeebies. Amy worked with Tom and the rest of the town's firefighters. Their attitudes and male viewpoints had rubbed off on her friend. She'd begun spouting male platitudes and using their logic more and more. Bunny wondered how far it would go.

She wasn't a tease, but seeing Brent's reaction as she leaned down to hand him his dessert was worth the trip back to the table. Setting the plate in front of him, she stood shaking a can of whipped cream. His sideways glance and quick nod said she had his attention.

"A little or a lot?" she asked, pointing the nozzle at the plate. If he waited too long to answer her, she'd have to shake the can again.

Brent picked up his fork. "Tell you what, make it to-go and I'll get it on my way out."

Bunny nodded and reached for the plate. Whipped cream shot out of the nozzle, landing short of the edge of the table.

"Whoa! Easy with that thing," he teased, grabbing his napkin and shielding his shirt.

"Sorry about that, Brent." She leaned toward him, reaching for the plate. If she bent any lower, she'd give him an eyeful. Oddly enough, she didn't mind and wished that more than the top two buttons of her embroidered white polo shirt were undone.

She straightened up and handed him his check. "Crisp is on the house. I'll have it waiting for you up front. Take your time."

She moved to the counter and propped her chin in her hands with a sigh. Business was good. Busy mornings serving breakfast and a lunch rush mixed with the takeout service kept her running until late afternoon. Dinnertime slowed as the seasons changed.

Brent rose, dusting his uniform pants free of lingering crumbs. She wondered if his briefs were regulation whites or if he pushed the line, choosing colored shorts or boxers. Brent's eyes rose. He caught her watching him. *Damn.* He tugged the pleats of each pant leg and picked up his check. She swallowed hard. He didn't divert his gaze as he walked to the cash register. Warmth crept up her neck and down toward her chest.

Kate, Bunny's eighteen-year-old daughter, burst through the kitchen door. "Mom, Max is here. We're going to the library. I'll be home late. Don't forget about cheerleading practice."

She kissed Bunny's cheek and ran out the door. Bunny stepped behind the register. Looking down, she saw Kate's backpack. "I swear that girl would forget her hind-end if it weren't tied on."

Brent chuckled. "What'd she forget this time?" He laid his check on the counter and started to hand Bunny his cash.

Bunny shook her head. "Her backpack and cheerleading uniform. She'll be back. Stand clear of the door."

Bunny retrieved the backpack and started toward the entry. Out of the corner of her eye, she saw motion. Waving her hand, she reached out. "Brent, look out!"

Too late! Kate heaved open the door. Its heavy metal edge caught Brent between the shoulders, pushing him into Bunny's arms. Kate's airborne backpack thudded near Tom's feet.

The pinging of change and rustling of bills followed as Bunny tried to back away from Brent. Strong hands stopped her. He held her at arm's length. His firm grip on her waist renewed the heat in her cheeks as she blushed. Her foot hit something. Glancing over her shoulder, she gulped, cornered between a man and the wall with nowhere to go. Concern gurgled below the surface of her uneasiness. This was too close.

Brent came closer. Mere inches from her; he cleared his throat and smiled. "Thanks for the warning, *Red*."

His hand lingered at her waist before patting her warm cheek. He nodded again and turned, his pelvis brushed against her hip. Heated stiffness blazed over her flesh and was gone. Had the man dragged his hard-on across her thigh? Bunny swallowed hard and raised her eyes.

Brent was gone. Two-way radio reverbs faded as squawks of words echoed. Sirens and the heavy motors of the fire trucks rattled the café's front window as they raced down the street.

* * * *

Soft keyboard strokes filled the quiet diner. Bunny sat in the front booth sipping coffee and added the day's receipts. Kate ate dinner in between doing her homework and writing an article for the school newspaper. Bunny looked up as loud racing engine sounds roared past the window.

Nine p.m. Brent and his crew returned from one more call. The past six hours consisted of two fires and three ambulance runs. Bunny wondered if they'd eaten. Getting up, she started towards the door. Red lights flashed, and alarms sounded. The loud speaker called out yet another run. Her eyes ran over the figures standing next to the lead truck.

Immediately, she found Brent. His six-foot-five-inch frame and short, tousled hair gave him away. He stood taller than most of his crew. Lights flashed across Brent's face. Smoke and soot decorated parts of his forehead and cheeks. Two more calls cascaded over the loud speaker. Bunny gripped her pencil tighter. It cracked between her fingers. She worked hard to dampen and push away her feelings. An all too familiar worry filled her, making her stomach knot with anxiety as she watched the weary firemen. Another long night of little sleep lay ahead of them.

* * * *

"What do you mean I have to be out by Friday?"

Brent crossed his eyes and sucked in air between his gritted teeth. Mrs. Stanford babbled on about how sorry she was. Shouldering his phone to his ear, he unclenched his hand to grab pen and paper. Ten minutes later, he had a list of phone numbers. His watch showed ten p.m. He'd worked twenty-four hours straight and was on call for two days next week. His answering machine flashed. Crap, what more could go wrong? He hit the play button.

"Hi, Brent! This is Marie Foster."

Great, what now did his realtor want? The house closing was scheduled for Tuesday. He hoped she had good news. Maybe he could get into the house earlier. Mrs. Stanford's suggestion of storage for his excess belongings as a temporary fix had possibilities.

"The house inspection went off without too many issues."

"Yes!" Brent whooped in elation as he smacked his kitchen table, rattling his coffee cup closer to the edge. Rolling his eyes heavenward, he mouthed a silent prayer. *Please let this work in my favor.*

"The inspector stated minor repairs need to be done to bring the house up to code. While he was under the house, he found bee and ant infestations. Fumigation is needed."

Okay, he understood that. A couple of days at best to spray the house and air it out. He could bunk at the firehouse. Nothing too bad. Marie's message went on.

"The wiring and plumbing will have to wait until the fumigation is done. The house has to be tented to ensure the bees are dead and the inside checked for nests. That delays things for at least ten days to two weeks. I've scheduled the exterminators for eight a.m. tomorrow."

"Shit!" Brent pushed against the precarious balance of the wobbly table. A loud crash followed. Hot coffee splattered on his bare feet. More curse words flew, and a lively dance ensued. Peanuts, his cat, perched atop the refrigerator, yowled in answer to Brent's cries of pain.

Even with a warm shower, some creative cussing, and a mug of Sleepy Time herbal tea, he laid in bed staring at the ceiling two hours later. Mrs. Stanford assured him he could get a few more days when he called to explain Marie's message. His options remained as before. Crash at the station indefinitely or find somewhere to live in the interim. His brain fogged, refusing to process coherent thoughts. His eyes drooped more with each breath. Beside him, Peanut's purrs stroked his ear. Sleep claimed him as his last thought fizzled out.

* * * *

Bunny stood in her driveway watching the McNeals pull away. Her last summer tenants were on their way home. Summer's receipts showed an unusual windfall. Finances were good for a while longer.

The jingle of the front door's bell alerted Bunny to an early-morning patron. Hanging her sweater on the coat pegs inside the café's kitchen, she donned her apron and called out. "I'll be there in a moment."

Who could it be? A quick glance at the wall clock showed six a.m. Since Brent's arrival, she'd lost track of the other firemen's schedules except his. Was Tom on cooking duty again? Had he burned the coffee again? He made a great assistant station commander, but couldn't cook worth crap. Had someone snuck over to get decent food and coffee?

"No rush," Brent's voice answered.

This was early by even Brent's standards. She knew his schedule as well as her own. Why was he at the firehouse on his day off? Something wasn't right.

She flicked on the second coffee maker and grabbed a pad and pen. "What'll it be…"

Her next words failed to vocalize. Brent sat two tables over, his faced buried in his hands. His uncombed hair and two-day beard growth showed around his cupped fingers. The man was a mess. She'd never seen him like this.

Grabbing two cups and the first brewed pot, she slid into the chair opposite him. "Here, hon, it's on the house."

* * * *

Brent peeked through his fingers. He breathed deeply. Fresh coffee wafted up each nostril. Heaven, sheer ecstasy after two days of

Tom's strong-enough-to-peel-paint percolations. Combing his hair with his hands, he smiled while Bunny poured. Three swallows later, he spoke.

"Thanks! You're a lifesaver. At least, Tom gets to live a while longer."

Bunny's short chuckle told him she wasn't buying his song and dance. Concern filled her eyes, yet she remained silent. She sipped her coffee and waited.

"Yeah, I look like hell. Feel like it, too." He shrugged, stirring his coffee and wondering how he could possibly explain his looks.

Dishes rattled in the kitchen, indicating Kate was awake. Soon smells of food cooking permeated the air. His stomach growled.

"Maybe some hot food would help?" Bunny's quiet question bought him a few more moments' reprieve. Nodding, he closed his eyes and swallowed more coffee. The scraping of chair legs and the sound of plates being set before him told him time was up.

Fluffy scrambled eggs and toast with homemade strawberry preserves and butter tantalized him. Hash browns just shy of overdone sat on a smaller plate nearby. His mouth salivated as he saw his normal order cooked to perfection. Days of warmed-up leftovers and stale coffee fled at his first bite. Fresh coffee filled his mug. One more thing caught his attention. Rivulets of sweat ran down the sides of the glass. Its cold, white filling temptingly beckoned. Bunny remembered his additional morning beverage. Ice-cold milk tasted sweeter than sugar going down his throat. He decided to let Tom live if he gave up cooking.

Bunny ate in companionable silence with him. Brent reached over and squeezed her hand. "Thanks for everything."

His radio drowned out her response. He unhooked it from his belt and barked out, "Brent here. I'm at Kater's. Tony's in charge. I'm off duty in five seconds. Over and out." He clicked off the ensuing chatter. "Now if I could just get a decent night's sleep, I might resemble a human."

* * * *

Bunny smiled. Personally familiar with firemen's harried, crazy schedules, she patted Brent's hand. "Been down that road a few times myself. A day off should help."

"I wish it were that simple. The on-call crew can't leave the station, and quarters are cramped. I haven't had time to set up my office, and it's even worse when it has to double as a bedroom."

"I guess you'll be heading home then. Drive carefully, and sleep well."

"I don't have to worry about driving. But, *sleep?* With all that racket?" He snorted. Traffic sounds and the squawk of the loudspeaker rushed through the opening door. Ben, the short order cook, nodded and entered the kitchen.

"I don't get it." Bunny paused. Brent's cryptic words didn't make sense. He couldn't sleep at the station given all the noise? His statement about not worrying about driving puzzled her the most.

"Remember the older house I bought last month?"

"Yes, you celebrated by buying dinner for the station. What's happened?"

"Bugs, drugs, and renters, oh my." His sheepish grin and shrug punctuated his words.

"Your apartment got rented, and the house has an issue with bugs?"

"Mrs. Stanford's son and daughter-in-law are moving back to town. She rented my place to them. They're due Friday. My house sits tented for another forty-eight hours. Extermination of bees and ants took more poison than expected."

"That's not good. When can you move into the house?"

"Three to four more weeks at the earliest. Repairs start next week to bring the house up to code. Forty-eight hours after they're done, I can officially move in furniture. Meanwhile, I've got to find a place to live instead of camping out at the station."

Kate whizzed through, stopping next to the table.

"Hi, Mr. Stephens. I overheard part of your conversation as I ate in the kitchen." She turned to Bunny. "Mom, he could stay here," she offered before rushing out.

* * * *

"Stay here?" Brent surveyed the room. The stairs near the front entrance lead to the upper level. He hadn't given much thought to them. He'd heard of folks renting rooms at Kater's and assumed it was the two additional rooms adjacent to Bunny's living quarters on the lower level. "Would that be all right?"

Bunny's laughter caught him by surprise. "Yes, it's fine. Come with me, and I'll show you what Kate was talking about."

Kater's Café took up the front half of her home. The restructured bed and breakfast had been a gem in the rough when she bought it. Made over into two duplexes by the prior owners, Bunny lovingly restored the inn to its former glory. The residents' rooms held renters during the summer months and a few local folks from time to time. The rear half housed her and Kate's living quarters. It comprised a medium-sized living room, four bedrooms, and two baths. Two of the four bedrooms stored her eldest children's cast offs.

At the top of the stairs, Brent found three doors. Bunny unlocked the one closest to her. She motioned him inside. A large, empty sitting room with an attached bath greeted him. Mustiness and dust tickled his nose.

Bunny struggled, opening two windows. Fresh air and sunlight filtered in. "I rent out these rooms during the summer to beach goers and local workers. Sometimes I have a tenant or two for the off-season. This room hasn't been used in a while. Since you need a place for an extended period, having your own things and some of your furniture around might help. As the others are furnished, this empty one might work better."

"I won't bother you with my late hours and weird schedule?"

"Nope, there are plenty of solid sound barriers between the front and back of this place. You'll have your own key. With the station next door, you can be there at a moment's notice. All I ask is that you have no wild parties or unwelcomed guests."

"What about Peanuts?"

"I don't tell my tenants what to eat, and as long as you clean up behind yourself, you can have all the peanuts you want."

Brent chortled. "Sorry, I meant my cat Peanuts."

Bunny grinned. "Sure, no issues provided he's fixed and won't be serenading all the females in the neighborhood."

Brent stuck out his hand. "Deal. And he's as docile as they come. Feed him and keep his box clean, and he's a gem."

Bunny wiped her sweaty palm on her rump. She took his hand. Why was her hand still sweaty? The hair on his arm stood up as static electricity sizzled up his arm.

"Ouch!" Bunny dropped his hand and stepped back from him. Her gaze around the room and slow retreat said something was up. Was she really that comfortable with him renting from her?

Chapter Two

"Careful, Tony. I can charge you for messing up my bed. Mar up Bunny's walls and the *county* pays," Brent joked.

Tony's deep laugh rolled out from under the mattress he carried. "Yeah, if it's anything like the paperwork to purchase the new coffee pot, Lord help us all."

Brent joined Tony's laughter. Convincing the county commissioner and the rest of county board why the station's old, corroded coffeemaker needed replacing had been a lesson in governmental paperwork. Brent better understood the city's tendency to acquire and seek reimbursement at budget hearings.

"Chief, it ain't none of my business. But *pink* walls?" Tony's exclamation echoed in the empty room.

"It's temporary, and it isn't any worse than the neon green paint in the break room."

Tony's sheepish grin peered over one end of the mattress he muscled across the room. "Okay. Okay. Next time I'll ask to see the color before I let the volunteers paint."

Brent shook his head. Tony's jovial nature was catching. The muffled sounds of his staff crept up the stairs.

"Up here, guys," he called out as he leaned out the window. Below he could see Bunny held the door and directed the men toward his room. He smiled at Peanuts and Bunny's interaction.

Peanuts, safe in his pet carrier, sat near her feet. An outstretched paw poked through the bars, patting her leg as if the cat sought reassurance. His marbled brown-tone coat resembled his namesake.

Patches of medium brown gave way to light tan offset by his white markings.

Brent located his pickup, empty of furniture and personal effects, parked next to Bunny's car and truck. Tom's car held the last few boxes waiting to be unloaded.

"Ms. Bunny," Tony yelled out as he made his way down the stairs. "Can you bring the cat up? Him and me don't get along too good."

"Be there in a moment," she replied. Brent watched as Bunny picked up the carrier and scratched Peanut's chin. Brent heard Bunny making her way up the stairs. He took inventory of his home for the next few weeks. Marie's latest call about the electrician possibly needing more time to bring the house up to code hadn't set well. He wondered about Bunny's reaction when she learned her new tenant might be staying longer.

He turned around as footsteps neared. Bunny, followed by Tom and Tony with the last few of his boxes, entered the room. "Thanks, guys. Are there anymore?"

"Just a couple more. Steve and Chuck will be up with them shortly. I can handle the late shift," Tom offered, moving toward the door.

Tony winked and sat his box near the open closet. "Yeah, Chief. Tom and I can oversee things for tonight. You need a chance to unpack and settle in. We know where you're at if we need you." He turned and nodded to Bunny as he followed Tom down the stairs.

Brent sat the carrier on the bed and let Peanuts out. He watched as the cat picked his way carefully across the bed heading to Bunny. Her hand motioned Peanuts closer. His low, rumbling purr began as she scratched and petted him. Brent caught her warm smile and relaxed posture. She liked cats, a definite plus in his book. Brent marveled at Peanut's next move.

He'd never seen the cat paw someone to ask for more attention. Brent took note of it He'd learned to trust Peanuts's reaction to people. Some considered it kooky. He didn't care. So far, Peanuts hadn't let him down.

"Yes, you're a good kitty." Bunny stroked Peanuts one more time before turning to Brent. "I'm sorry for the lack of decorating touches. This room gets used more for storage than anything else."

"No problem," Brent began as Chuck and Steve topped the stairs. Their conversation drowned out his next words.

"What do you mean the quarterback needs glue on his hands?" Steve's voice carried through the open door.

Chuck's deep laugh and snort echoed up the stairs, and his reply mixed with the lingering noise. Steve entered first, his response booming off the boxes he carried.

"Sorry, Ms. Bunny," Steve said, lowering his voice. "These are the last ones, Chief."

Chuck grinned and placed his box next to Brent's dresser. Steve sat his on top and turned to leave.

"Wait one minute, guys." Brent stepped toward them. "Give me one of your radios, and tell Tony he's to call me at the end of his shift."

Steve unclamped his from his belt and handed it to Brent. "Will do. Night, Ms. Bunny."

* * * *

"Good night." Bunny smiled at their departing lower-toned conversation as they descended the stairs.

Brent sat on the one clear spot in the room—his bed. He patted the small, empty space next to him. "Have a seat."

Bunny's throat went dry. She tried swallowing, creating a dry, hacking cough. She cleared her throat and ran the tip of her tongue over her lips. Her heart raced and pounded. It'd been a while since a man had offered her such a seat. She doubted he meant anything by it. *Did he?*

"My two folding chairs are stuffed in the back of the closet. My father would haunt me if I continued to let you stand." He smiled, moving over to create more room.

Why did she feel dizzy? She inhaled, reminding herself to breathe. Her head clearing, she perched on the edge of the bed.

Brent shifted, positioning himself toward her. She watched his mattress roll and pitch like waves along the shore. Her high-pitched squeak broadened Brent's smile. More ripples and waves moved her closer to him.

"Sorry," he began steadying her with his hands, "the mattress isn't fully inflated."

"Inflated?"

"Yes, a combination of air and inner spring technology. Let's me adjust it for comfort. More air firmer, less air softer, resting on springs." He held up the Sleep Number bed's pump and gauge control.

Relief washed over Bunny. Yet, a bubble of disappointment popped when she realized he wasn't making a pass at her. Shaking her head, she sat back, anchoring herself with her hands.

"Something wrong?" Brent's question caught her off guard.

"Uh-h-h-mm no. Just thinking about your unique mattress." His raised eyebrows and incredulous look quieted her.

"Is it ok if I hang some pictures? Maybe some drapes?"

"Quite a bit for a few weeks."

Brent grinned wryly and shrugged. "I may be staying longer."

"Longer?" Not that it was a problem. She had other rooms available. Still, the idea of his being around longer set off a bouncing ping in a few different directions.

"Possibly. My contractor may need longer to complete the upgrades and inspections."

His intent gaze unnerved her. She knew he wanted an answer. Did she have one? Uncertainty mired her thoughts. Her location next to the firehouse worked from a business aspect. It provided her a steady stream of patrons and made her easy to locate. She felt safe knowing someone was always close by. Help was a few steps away. That was prior to Brent and before she began to feel again. Unsure how to respond, she rocked forward.

Her movement set the mattress in gear, undulating and pitching its occupants in various directions. Brent lunged toward her, his hands open. Peanut's angry yowl and hiss signaled his rapid departure.

One ripple after another tossed them closer. She tried to counter the movement, thinking its force would cancel her shift. No such luck! She bumped Brent's shoulder. She pushed back, hoping to separate them.

* * * *

"Ouch!" Brent rubbed his shoulder, and reaching with his free hand, he grabbed for her. Soft flesh filled his palm. He quit looking for Peanuts and glanced sideways. Bunny reeled toward him.

"Hey! Look out!"

Her warning came too late. All motion ceased. Their heavy breathing sizzled the air. Two prone bodies lay atop the bed. Bunny precariously covered him.

Brent peered over her shoulder and looked down toward the end of the bed. "Great," he muttered. A tangle of legs and clothing along with other snarled body parts greeted him.

His hand, tangled in between their bodies, held her breast. Wiggling his fingers, cloth moved, exposing warm flesh. He pulled upward. Her sharp intake stopped him. She tried rising up. Brent groaned. "Watch your knee!"

He tugged and pulled, working to free his hand. A rip sounded. His movement halted. Jerking produced further thread popping sounds and a moan of pain from Bunny. "You all right?"

"No. Your watch is caught on my bra," she whispered. "Every time you pull or move sharply, it binds tighter around me. One good yank and you'll have my bra and shirt on your wrist."

Brent slid his hand side to side. His fingers brushed the lace-covered underside of her breasts. Her pebbling nipples accented the heated undertones building between them. Filing away her reaction, Brent paused. How did he get them apart?

"Can you roll on your side?"

Bunny's wide-eyed look said he needed to explain.

"When I slide my hand back and forth, there's some give. If we lie side by side, we might be able to work my watch free."

Bunny moved, bringing her knee closer to his cock and balls. "Slow down," he ground out, afraid to breathe with her bent leg a hair's width away. "We've got to do this together."

With Bunny's silent nod, he continued.

"Stretch your leg out, and swing it over mine so you're straddling me."

Each movement drove his cock to hotter hardness. He didn't dare speak as he fought for control. He hadn't planned to do the Latin Sizzle prone on a bed. He preferred his dirty dancing naked and without distractions.

Bunny stopped as she straddled him. A sheet of paper couldn't fit between them. Her pelvis and hips lay tight against his. Each time she breathed, he swore their combined internal heat raged higher.

She raised her head and licked her lips. Her gaze roved over his face. Her deepened eye color indicated her apparent arousal.

"Wrap your arms around my neck, and rise up on your knees as best you can."

Her next move edged his control close to nil. Her rocking pelvis chafed his growing hardness. Too much more and he'd come. Gritting his teeth, he ground out their next action.

"Roll to the right with me when I say. One, two, three...go!"

They moved in one fluid motion. Bunny's leg lay trapped under his. His knee rested between her thighs, nudging closer to her crotch. Her other leg dangled over his hip.

"Your…umm…wrist is free. Your watch is another thing."

"What do you mean?" Brent asked, pulling his arm from between them. Grabbing her shirt hem, he yanked it rib high. His watchband greeted him. Loosening his grip, he tugged her collar to him. Unprepared for the sight within, he damn near creamed his pants.

His watch lay nestled between her partially covered breasts. Torn lace caught on her thick, engorged nipples, standing firmly erect. If he didn't stop gawking, he'd be in real trouble. Maybe give in to his urge to taste them. He could imagine their flavor rolling across his tongue.

Feeling something touch his cheek, he brushed at it and raised his head. A solid *thunk* rumbled near his ear. Garbled cries of pain greeted him. Tilting his head back, he realized his oops. Bunny moved her jaw back and forth, puckering her lips. Temptation refused any more denial.

He cupped her chin and held firm. "I'll kiss the hurt away," he murmured and caught her bottom lip between his. He sucked gently, pulling its plumpness into his mouth. The edge of his teeth nibbled her lip's fullness.

Slowly, his tongue outlined the boundary of her upper lip. He ventured inward, tasting and savoring her flavor. He showered kisses down her chin, pausing briefly to reassure her.

"Easy, sweetie. You're okay."

* * * *

His hoarse tone brushed along Bunny's jaw, rising to warm her ears. His soft, hissed "Yes," drew her awareness outward. His forehead rested against hers. Through semi-closed eyes, she saw her mirrored desire.

A golden glow flashed across his pupils. The spark flared brighter as her hand stroked his cheek. Her fingertips brazed over his strong jaw line, adding fuel to her inner vision of his strength of character. His firm, masculine mouth and chiseled jaw complemented his warm, tender eyes. Bunny sighed, returning his earlier shared warmth.

Brent angled his head and pressed home. Her opened mouth "ooh" permitted him entrance. He boldly entered, his tongue seeking hers. She nipped his, shyly seeking her own draught to quench her thirst. He withdrew, igniting the chase.

She followed deep into his lair. Her tongue silkily caressed and tasted him. Her hands gripped his shoulders then hooked around his neck. He held the back of her neck and tangled his fingers in her hair. Their tongues mated with their craving.

Brent pulled back. Slipping his arms lower, he created space between them. "Wow," he whispered and wet his lips. Bunny's eyes met his and lowered immediately. He worked to bring her gaze back to him. "Hey, you okay?"

Her head bobbed even though her focus refused to meet his. She hoped he didn't take her silence and heavy breathing as embarrassment even though she was. She could handle a few hot kisses. *Couldn't she?*

"Come on. Please talk to me," he said.

"I need to get downstairs before Kate gets home. We'll talk later." Bunny pushed against him, moving away. She glanced at him before slipping out the door. He'd gotten to her as much as she had him.

Chapter Three

"Hi, Mr. Stephens." Brent's startled jump brought a smile and giggles to Kate. "Sorry. Ben said to get your order."

Brent scanned the menu. Hunger had driven him to seek food, but something else drove him to Kater's instead of the cookout on the station's back patio. He looked around the almost-empty dining area. Only a few late lunch goers occupied with their chatter and meals caught his eye. A quick glance toward the kitchen revealed nothing that he hadn't already figured out. Bunny was either busy in her office or out. He'd gotten familiar with her comings and goings in the three weeks he'd been staying there.

"I'll have some of your mom's meatloaf with mashed potatoes and plenty of gravy. Fresh coffee and a large milk." Handing Kate the menu, he voiced the one question he didn't want to ask. "Where's your mom?"

No sooner had he spoken than he realized his error. Verbalizing his curiosity was one thing. Saying it aloud to a teenager and the daughter of his strong interest was another. He hoped Kate didn't read more into his question.

"Mom's off with Amy, celebrating her birthday prematurely. They went to a spa for the day."

Kate walked away and halted. She turned back, watching him. A decisive look briefly passed over her face before she shook her head.

Brent sighed as Kate clipped his order to the menu board near Ben. For a moment, he'd sworn she knew the reason behind his question. If he'd known before what he knew now, he would've kissed Bunny sooner. He didn't understand why she'd avoided him for the better part of a week. Her response said she was affected, too.

Silverware rattled, jolting him back to the present. Kate placed his coffee and milk center of the table. "Ben said it'll be a couple more minutes. Enjoy your salad and rolls." Kate didn't move away.

She fingered two turned-up pages of her order pad. She glanced nervously toward the front tables and rubbed her lips together.

"Kate, is something wrong?"

"Mr. Stephens, I want to know..." The scraping of chairs quieted her. The last two patrons left, leaving Kate and him.

"Sit down, Kate. I'm sure Ben will call when my order's ready."

Kate slid into the seat opposite him. She leaned forward, her hands and order pad on the table.

"Mom's birthday is four days from now. Amy, Ben, and I are planning her surprise party. Most of the town is in on it."

Brent continued eating his salad in silence, wondering what Kate was working up to. He nodded, waiting for her to go on.

"Ben forgot to invite the fire station. Please say you'll come."

He saw the list of names as Kate folded back the pages of her order pad. He estimated about twenty-five names per sheet on the three she flipped through, far more than Kater's could comfortably fit and an amount that pushed the fire code's capacity allowance.

"Order up!"

Kate slid to the edge of her seat. She reached for her pad. "Leave it," Brent countered. "I'll have an answer for you in a moment."

She rose and walked away but not before an anxious glance passed over her face. Brent knew his answer before she returned. He wondered about Bunny's reaction when they came face to face again, this time in front of the whole town. Let her try to avoid him.

Kate set Brent's meal down. Brent placed his hand on hers.

"I'll come with one stipulation. You use the station's patio and facilities. It'll be our gift to Bunny. No muss. No fuss."

A hundred-watt smile beamed across Kate's face. "Thank you, Mr. Stephens! Mom will be really surprised."

Brent watched Kate bounce off. Four days to get Bunny a gift. He wasn't sure he could pull it off. An idea formed that had him grinning and planning.

* * * *

"Pink or fuchsia?" Amy asked, holding two bottles of nail lacquer. "Maybe both? Alternate every other nail?" She turned and burst out laughing. She wished she had a camera. Talk about a Kodak moment! Bunny's bug-eyed "you've got to be kidding" look sent the manicurist and two patrons into fits of amusement.

"Cool out, girlfriend," Amy spit out between peals of laughter. "I'm joking. Besides, only my tootsies get any color. Regulations and restrictions." Amy wiggled her toes and spread them as her attendant rubbed her feet.

"Ma'am, the masseur is ready for you." The receptionist held out a towel and robe to Bunny.

"Can you behave?" Bunny asked, pointing to Amy. "Or do I remain to chaperone?"

"Go on, birthday girl. Get them kinks smoothed out. I'll be along in a few. Love those pale peach French tips. Good choice."

Bunny draped the robe and towel over her arm. Following the masseur to the locker room, she smiled. Amy's gift had been a definite surprise.

Entering the small changing area, Bunny caught her reflection in the full-length mirror outside of the shower cubicle. She didn't feel or look a day over forty. What did forty-six look and feel like?

Her nipples pointed out, despite being baby used. Turning sideways, her waist didn't need sucking in. Her tush rounded in all the right places. She took care of herself.

She remembered her mom's fortieth and fiftieth birthdays. Mom's favorite saying was "age is just a number." She'd out-danced and out-done folks five years younger than her. It was at times like this that Bunny missed her the most.

A knock broke her train of thought. "Ready, ma'am?" her masseur called out.

Bunny stuffed her clothes into the locker and closed it. Wrapping the bathrobe securely around her, she slipped her feet into her flip-flops. She exited and followed the short hall to the room where the masseur waited.

The massage table sat in the center of the well-lit room with sliding glass doors along one wall. Natural light peeked through the partially closed blinds covering the frosted panes. Soft classical music filled the air, and the incense of her choice burned nearby. She sat on the table, watching as he mixed and warmed her oils.

"Do you have any particular spots or areas that need work?"

Bunny hesitated. Her shoulders, feet, and legs knotted after a day on her feet and hours serving. Working the kinks out usually consisted of a soak in the tub when time permitted. Why not enjoy Amy's gift and let a professional soothe her taut, stressed muscles?

"My legs, feet, and shoulders are my problems areas."

"Please lie down on your stomach, and drape the sheet around your waist. I'll work on your shoulders first, finishing with a hot rock treatment along your lower back. Then I'll rub down your legs and feet. If you like, I can end with your arms and hands as you lay on your back fully covered."

Bunny nodded and lay with her face in the open pillow cradle, looking at the floor. She smirked at the fake mosaic tiles littering the floor. One particular picture intrigued her. It reminded her of the shoreline where she and Derrick honeymooned.

Warm oil poured across her shoulders and pooled in the small of her back. Strong male hands pressed and rubbed deep into her stressed, tight muscles. A sense of well-being and peace lulled her into a hazy, daydreaming snooze. Tired of fighting her conscience, she let her mind wander where it wanted, down memory lane.

College sweethearts, she and Derrick married soon after his graduation from the firefighters' academy. EMT certification hadn't been enough for him. He had to be a firefighter, too. He wanted to be in the action, saving lives on the front line, not from the sidelines.

Things had gone along great until the kids came along shortly afterwards. Derrick's preoccupation with money and giving them the best drove them to several large cities, Richmond being their last. Derrick's untimely death had sent her running south and east, dragging two toddlers and her unborn child with her.

Tears pricked her eyes. She fought them back. The past was over, and rehashing it did no good. Today was for and about her. She'd be damned if she'd let Derrick rob her of her peace of mind and tranquility after all this time. Repeating her twenty-year-old mantra, she forced herself to breathe deeply and let go. *Look forward and not back. Ahead is your course, and you are in charge.* Now if her stubborn conscience would listen, she'd be able to calm down and enjoy the massage. Soon her breathing slowed, and she drifted into a relaxed state. Bunny turned off her internal monitor and sank into a light sleep.

She jolted upward. Cool air surged down her neck and over her exposed back and shoulders.

"Sorry, ma'am," the masseur said. "The fan blew the heated sheet off you. Your friend awaits you in the whirlpool."

Bunny hastily changed into her traditional two-piece bathing suit. Amy chided her conservative swimwear. Her figure might support bikinis, but her courage didn't. A two-piece was as bold as she got.

A quick look in the mirror revealed a woman who didn't look any different than she had six years earlier on her fortieth birthday. So why did she feel as though change's elusive lure dangled before her, waiting to ensnare her within its web?

If change wanted her, she was ready. Hell, who was she trying to fool? Much of her life felt comfortable and fit, like a worn pair of shoes. Since Brent's arrival, she'd started seeing and sensing things with a new perspective and interest. Or, was it because it was her birthday? Either way, things were different.

One last look in the mirror and a wink, she smiled knowing that Amy was right. Spa days and birthdays deserved extravagances of some sort. Lunch with Amy at the spa's new in-pool bar area awaited her. Sitting at a bar while in the pool, much less eating, seemed odd. Who said indulgences had to fit within one's comfort zones? Well, outside them a bit was okay, right?

"Here's to you." Amy raised her long-stemmed glass. Its pale gold fluid bubbled and gave off a tart odor like its alcoholic counterpart. "May your birthday bring you joy and presents extraordinaire."

Her wink and sassy grin caused Bunny to choke. Thank God, they were drinking carbonated apple juice and not expensive champagne.

"Any plans for the actual day?" Amy asked.

Bunny waited before answering, enjoying her salad. Relaxed and de-stressed, along with lunch while enjoying the whirlpool, capped the day.

"A quiet dinner with Kate and a DVD. You're welcome to join us."

"I just might."

* * * *

Brent closed his office door. Sitting at his desk, he drew the FedEx envelope from under his blotter. He slit it open. Three envelopes fell out as he up-ended it. He smiled. Randy had come through for him. That left one item unfinished. Brent unsealed the one bearing his name. He read the letter within.

You asked for a venue close to home. Birthdays are reasons to celebrate and do it up right. Before you start fussing, read further.

My wife's boss gets season tickets, and he offered his private seats at no additional charge. We'll be out of town ourselves, so our penthouse hotel suite in town is available. What does this mean?

You and your guest have reservations at Le Grande on Times Square. Following dinner, as per your request and as guests of Cupertino Corporation, enjoy the Broadway production of Cats. The Ritz Times Square awaits your late-night slumber and rest. You can check in anytime and stay as long as you like. There is no charge beyond your nominal expenses.

A night on the town deserves New York, and what better place to celebrate a birthday? I miss you, bro. Wish we were going to be around to meet the lucky lady. Mom sends her love as does Grandma. Love ya!

Randy

P.S. Mom says come home soon for a visit!

Brent folded the letter. Tears pricked his eyes. His family was unique. They feuded and fussed constantly. Their strong-willed personalities stood rock firm and saw them through many of life's hardships. Two things endured no matter what—their love and respect for each other and their genuine commitment to remaining connected as a family. He missed them.

He wasn't sure how much of his past continued to haunt him. The blue September sky that day that ended in ashes would be with him forever, but the flashbacks had eased off, the pain muffled by time and work. Diving back into work and accepting the promotion to captain had helped healing begin. Things had changed when he hit forty, and now two years later, he wanted something more. But, was he ready to return to New York and Ground Zero? He'd soon be finding out.

Chapter Four

Brent lifted the bag of charcoal off his shoulder. Three half-barrel barbecues stood in the middle of the brick patio. Fire extinguishers sat nearby.

"Hey, Chief. Folks are asking where to park."

Brent turned. Tom stood behind Tony. Each wore slogan-marked aprons. Tom's fit his cooking abilities. It read, "I'm a good cook. NOT!" A large black circle with a diagonal line through it overlay good. Tony's quirky sense of humor showed with his "Kiss the Cook. Please?"

"Tom, get Chuck and Steve to pull the trucks and ambulance close to the street. Leave the garage doors open. Kate and Amy took Bunny to Blockbuster on a pretense of renting movies."

Tom left, barking orders into his walkie-talkie. He called back over his shoulder. "Parking?"

"Use the drugstore's lot two blocks over. Gotta have some element of surprise."

Tony stepped closer. "Tom's a great assistant chief. Hope he works out as cook's assistant."

"Ben will help you with the grills. He's bringing the meat and sodas." Brent pulled two sheets of paper from his shirt pocket. "Okay, parking is taken care of. Get Dave and Kingston to load washtubs with ice, soda, and bottled water. Anyone seen drinking alcohol is out of here. We're on duty. No booze allowed."

Tony nodded and pointed. Brent followed Tony's finger. Ben and several neighbors exited the firehouse carrying large ice chests. "Okay, Tony, you're on."

Brent walked toward the station. He noticed the colorful decorations outlining the backdoor. Several locals busied themselves moving tables and chairs. Many greeted him by name as he entered. Before going to his office, he glanced through the two large rear windows. He marveled at the number of folks assisting and arriving. This was a community event. Jameston wasn't New York. A shiver inched down his spine, warming by the time it reached the small of his back. He knew he'd made a good choice in coming here.

* * * *

"Come on, Mom." Kate fussed, tugging at Bunny's arm. "We've got two movies. Let's go."

"Yeah, let's go. My crock-pot stew will be ready by the time we get back." Amy checked her watch. "A girl needs to keep up her strength."

Bunny took in the two grinning faces before her. Kate had surprised her with breakfast in bed. Amy had already gifted her. She'd never known Kate to choose a movie so quickly. She'd go along with them. God help them if they hired a stripper!

Amy drove past the station and parked in Bunny's driveway. "The trucks are out. Everyone's inside. I better see what's up."

"What about your stew?" Bunny asked, pausing as she unlocked her door.

"It'll be fine. Come with me. Brent mentioned some papers he had for you from your last inspection."

Bunny followed in Amy's wake, praying Brent wouldn't mention their kiss.

The crowd parted as they entered. Two air-horn blasts shrieked out of the loud speakers. Confetti filled the air amidst yells of "Surprise!"

Amy pushed Bunny forward. People parted more. Drumbeats began, followed by rhythmic handclaps. Someone stepped forward.

Kate grabbed one arm, Amy the other. They spun her around to face the front of the station.

Three muscular firemen with hard, six-pack abs, and covered by the skimpiest shorts she'd ever seen, strutted towards her. Each wore a banner similar to a beauty queen's sash. Kingston's read "Happy". Steve's read "Birthday". And Brent's read "Bunny".

"All right, gentlemen!" Amy called out, punching the air. Music keyed through the loud speaker.

Bunny staggered. *No, they weren't going to...were they?* David Rose's 'The Stripper" began to play. Someone guided her into a chair. Fake dollar bills filled her hands. She scanned the crowd, looking for Kate or Amy. She caught glimpses of them as the women in the crowd moved forward and the men back. Movement toward the open front drew her attention.

The music changed beat, mixing with the rancorous female yells. The opening lyrics of "Save a Horse, Ride a Cowboy" boomed out. Kingston donned his Stetson and danced closer. He pulled the brim lower, shading his eyes. A saucy wink followed. Bumping and grinding his abs and hips, he inched nearer. He lowered one side of his waistband and spun, bringing his hips quite close. A hand grabbed a fake bill and stuffed his waistband.

"Come on, honey." Amy's voice crooned in her ear. "Join the fun. The fake bills get replaced with regular currency, and it goes to the children's hospital."

Bunny blinked twice. She recognized the hand pulling the note from hers. *Kate!* Her eighteen-year-old daughter!

She watched, slack jawed, as Kingston tipped his hat to Kate and two-stepped across the garage bay with her. Several bills hung from his low-hung shorts. Bunny sucked in air. The man could do one hell of a dirty shimmy.

Steve took short turns spinning and dipping ladies around the garage in tango dance moves. His decorated waist matched Kingston's as he blew kisses to the crowd. He stopped and took

Bunny's hand, kissing her wrist before offering her his arm. Chants and hand clapping began, growing in volume.

"Go for it!" rang out. Someone tipped her chair forward. She rose to keep from falling. Steve took her arm, steadying her, and entwined it with his. He stepped forward, propelling her with him. He assumed the opening tango dance position. Bunny faced him, unsure what to do. Brent strolled toward them.

The upper body of her dreams withered and died as reality replaced it. Fantasy couldn't live up to what she stared at. The man's pecs and abs were tight and firm in all the right places. A light dusting of brown hair decorated his arms and chest. She followed its trail downward toward. . . *Oh Lord.* At the rate she was going, she would have Brent stripped. Well, at least mentally, he would be. She tugged the neck of her shirt and raised her gaze. *Damn!* His semi-grin and cheeky wink said "Caught ya!" He adjusted his sash, pulling the tip of it out of his waistband. The movement caught her off guard. A peek below said more of the hair trail waited exploration. She gulped and found her throat dryer than her mouth. Did he have to tighten the sash as he moved, emphasizing his broad, well-built torso even more?

He tapped Steve's shoulder and pointed to her. Steve bowed to her and placed her hand in Brent's. Nat King Cole's duet version of "Unforgettable" with his daughter, Natalie, filled the air.

Brent spun Bunny close and began slow dancing around the bay. As the music faded, he hugged her. Firm flesh rippled under her hands and fingers. Warmth shot up her arms and pooled deep within her ribcage. It felt right, and yet it didn't. Brent's low "Thank you" whispered against her ear.

His hands rubbed from her tense shoulders to her lower back, stopping short of her waist. Her nipples tightened and budded, tenting her already tight shirt. He stepped sideways, taking her with him and turning them so his firm ass faced the crowd. She halted her fluttering hands as beads of perspiration formed beneath them. If she lowered them any farther, she'd be cupping him in a rather intimate way. Still, reality was proving much better than fantasy. Her hands fell to his waist just short of the top of his shorts. He wiggled and tensed his buttocks, causing her hands to slip under the edge of his waistband.

A loud wolf whistle split the air.

"Wooohoooo! Older woman, younger man!"

* * * *

Bunny tried pulling away. Brent held her tight and fast. "Stay put. Don't let them know they affected you."

Bunny titled her head back. Fear rushed through her eyes. His ego crashed deep into the pit of burning anxiety building in his gut. Stepping back a bit more, he created space between them, hoping she'd begin to calm down. Tears glistened her long lashes. He felt her tremble with each breath. He reassured her in the only way he knew how. His lips captured hers. As fast as it began, he broke away.

Taking her hand, he turned to the crowd. "Everyone dance and enjoy. Happy birthday, Bunny!" Applause and whistles followed, soon covered by music.

Brent tugged Bunny's hand. "Come with me." He nodded toward his office. At her scared rabbit look, he added, "Please?"

He closed the door behind them. "I want to give you my gift privately." He opened his middle desk drawer. Pulling out a large mauve-colored envelope, he pointed to his desk chair. "Have a seat. This will take a moment."

Brent pulled his uniform pants from a nearby chair. "Go ahead and open it while I change." His shirt hung on the open door to his bathroom.

He heard paper tear and a soft gasp. "I'll be out in a moment." He wasn't sure how to take her reaction. Was she surprised? Happy? Dismayed? He reached to open the door. It was too quiet.

She raised her face. Tears slowly slid down her cheeks. Her lips trembled. She shook her head as she mouthed "no". Brent placed his fingers to her mouth. He brushed his lips against hers. "Think about it. *Please.*" Picking up the contents of the envelope, he placed them in her hands. He cracked the door as the loud speaker crackled and began squawking with a call. "We have a connection I'd hate to lose." His lips swept hotly across hers.

Racing out the door, he called for assistance. They quickly donned their gear. Tom and Charlie, along with four others, raced toward the trucks at the end of the drive. Kingston and Steve ran toward the ambulance.

Brent lingered at the bay door watching Bunny intently as he waited for the others to join him. She stepped into the bay and wrapped her arms tightly around herself, fingering the envelope she held. Kate, wearing Kingston's Stetson, came up to her and draped her arm around Bunny's waist. Hugging her close, Kate spoke. Had he read her lips correctly *Mom, this isn't Dad. Brent will be back?*

* * * *

Brent lay staring at the ceiling, recalling the evening. Sleep eluded him. Two back-to-back calls had left him little time to enjoy the party. By the time he returned, the festivities were winding down.

Tony's foresight and organizational skills corralled Brent a late evening meal. Two well-done burgers slathered with Tony's homemade, sweet Carolina barbecue sauce, cheese, lettuce, and tomato hit the spot. Nibbling on his mixture of chips and pretzels, he sat watching the few remaining stragglers help clean up. Amy trotted over near him, dressed in her jogging clothes.

Sweat trickled down her face. He handed her a paper towel and moved over. "Care to sit?"

Her eyes narrowed as she wiped her face. The frown forming across her mouth didn't look inviting. He offered her the unopened water bottle sitting next to him.

"Why the look?" he asked, picking up his soda.

Amy plopped down across from him. She opened the bottle and downed half. "Chief, I may be out of line, but what the hell is going on with you and Bunny?"

"Amy, if it were anyone else, I'd tell you it's none of your damn business, but Bunny is your best friend. I appreciate your concern. What's eating you?"

Amy arched an eyebrow at him. A silent message rolled between them. He wasn't spilling more, and she wanted more. They sat staring at each other. After Amy finished her water, she sighed.

"Amy, if you've got something to say, spill it."

Amy opened her mouth. Brent held up his hand. "I'm not discussing personal details. That's between Bunny and me."

Amy wet her lips and stood. "Brent, Bunny's wellbeing and friendship mean a lot to me. I don't want to see her hurt. She's had enough pain in her life."

"Enough pain?"

"Past suffering and sorrow along with a few younger men and their indecisiveness. It's not mine to share. I don't know your intentions. Just be sure you are upfront with her. Don't hurt her, okay?"

Brent grasped Amy's arm as she turned to leave. "Amy, thanks for caring. Know Bunny's wellbeing matters to me, too. Good night."

Brent gathered his trash and tossed it in the barrel outside the rear door. He waved to Tom. Tom met him midway to his office.

"Chief, go home, and get some rest. Tony's going to be a while longer cleaning up. I'll take your shift."

"Thanks, Tom. Be sure to get some rest yourself. You've been on twelve hours straight."

"As soon as the coals are cool, Tony and I are lights outs."

Brent grinned at Tom's mock salute. Wearily, he walked down the drive. He glanced to Bunny's back windows. No lights. She was probably asleep. His watch showed twelve-thirty a.m.

His pace slowed as he fingered his keys. His shoulders ached, and his feet dragged with each step he took. Sleep threatened to claim him where he stood. Yawning, he unlocked the entry to the upstairs. A flash of light caught his attention. Was someone in there? A fire? Adrenaline kicked in.

* * * *

Bunny sat two booths back from the front door. Sleep refused to visit. Counting sheep irritated her as much as her growing fears and uneasiness at her reactions to Brent. The glass of warm milk she sipped wasn't helping, either. She smothered a yawn. Her body craved rest. Her restless mind said no.

Metal meeting metal jingled. Bunny watched as shadows danced along the small entry area separating the outside door from both inside ones, Kater's and the upstairs rooms. Light flashed over Brent's face. He shielded his eyes as car lights hit his face. His beard stubble and tousled hair indicated the length of his day. His weariness shone in his dropping eyelids.

She'd given him keys to both doors, instructing him to raid the refrigerator as needed if he worked past closing. Poor man was bone tired and ready to drop. Part of her conscience warred with her gut. A strong desire to let him get closer and nurture their growing connection fought past experience warning her to stay away. Did she want another Derrick? And their age difference, how bad was it?

She'd tried dating older and younger men. Younger men left her wanting and needing, not sexually, but rather emotionally. Older men offered an emotional connection, but often lacked interest in sexual needs or shared pursuits. She wanted a partner, someone who complemented her and she them. Mutual respect was essential.

Some younger men wanted a family and not necessarily a ready-made one like hers. Older gents--they were done with the child rearing part of their life. A few were looking for someone to replace their late spouse or caretaker. She didn't want more kids nor was she ready to be a live-in caretaker.

The front door clicked open. She slipped down in the seat, hoping to hide. She heard his keys hit the floor. Brent's soft "damn" made her smile. His further muttering brought giggles. Had they landed beneath the sharp edge of the double-tiered newspaper stand?

Light flooded the room. She blinked and shielded her eyes, closing them due the brightness.

Footsteps told her he approached. She ducked her head and tried slipping lower. Soon she'd end up wedged beneath the table. How was she going to get out?

No sound. Her eyes flew open. Was he in the kitchen? Could she sneak past him out the door marked private and into her office that connected to her home? Raising her head, she gulped.

He stood staring at her. Arms folded, keys dangling from his cut fingers—shit, they had landed under the newsstand—and his tightly drawn lips didn't spell out joy. His furled brow and hardened stance added emphasis she was quickly feeling uncomfortable about.

She pulled a napkin from the dispenser and handed it to him. "How bad is it?" She refused to look beyond his hands. Small cuts crisscrossed his three longest fingers on each hand. Blood beaded in tiny amounts on both.

"I'll live." He slid into the seat next to her, blocking any chance of escape. Her heavy sigh filled the small space between them. She scooted back, retreating until the sidewall prevented her movement.

"Damn it, woman, I thought you were a burglar." His harsh tone and curse ripped across her ears. He reached toward her. She jumped.

"Relax. I need another napkin." He pulled the dispenser to him. Wrapping two napkins around each of his fingers, he asked, "Do you have a first-aid kit?"

"Behind the register. I'll get it."

"*No*, I'll get it." His command startled her. Where did he get off ordering her around?

His stiff stance as he glared at her sent icy tingles along her shoulders. He turned away and shook his head.

* * * *

Brent moved to get the first-aid kit. He kept looking back, daring her to move. They needed to talk, and he was in no mood for games. He hated dishonest communication and avoidance. He'd gone through it enough in his marriage and a few past relationships. This time, he wasn't going to let it happen.

He bent down, reaching for the kit. Scraping sounded. He bolted upright. He caught her inching closer to the bench's edge. "Going somewhere?" He plopped the kit on the counter, glaring at her.

Her eyes darted back and forth from him to behind him. "Whatever you're planning, forget it."

Bunny's shrug and growing pile of shredded napkins tugged at his conscience. He was too tired and frustrated to play a cat and mouse game. Considering the mood he was in, she'd find out how quick his reflexes were and what a firemen's carry was all about. Images of her shapely derriere draped over his shoulder formed. Talk about access. His hormones shot into overdrive thinking about the pats and fondles along with a few well-placed nips he could do.

Dropping the kit on the table, he plopped into the seat opposite her. He pushed the kit to her. It stopped partway. A half-filled glass of milk impeded its movement.

"Clean my cuts, and talk while you're doing it. Why are you avoiding me?"

Chapter Five

Bunny pulled the kit to her. Anger simmered just below the surface. She didn't like his tone. He initiated both kisses, and curiosity had gotten the better of her. Okay, he got her stirred up real good. The man could kiss. How dare he act like it was all her fault?

Tearing open an antiseptic wipe, she assessed his hands. Several nicks covered his fingers. Dried flecks of blood indicated the minor lacerations. She swallowed hard, remembering the feather-soft caresses those fingers were capable of doing. Their strength saved lives daily. She touched Brent's palm. Tingles surged up her arm. His hand tightened over hers. Some of her anger dissipated.

His ragged sigh pulled her from her thoughts. "I can't force you to talk. I give up."

Bunny leaned forward and whispered. "My turn to kiss and make it better." She quickly brushed her lips over each hurt finger. She raised her eyes. "Thank you."

"For what?'

"For caring, for keeping an eye out for me, and my birthday celebration."

"You're welcome." He reached for the discarded wipe.

"Let me," she offered. Seeing his hesitation, she added, "Please?"

She began cleaning the cuts. She knew she couldn't hide from herself or her feelings any longer. Maybe getting things out in the open would set things right. Maybe it wouldn't. Either way, they had a while before sleep would come.

"Thanks for kissing my pain away." Brent withdrew his hand from hers. He wiped each finger, inspecting the size of the nicks and cuts. "I don't get it. When I try to get closer, you retreat. Care to explain?"

Bunny pushed away her pile of shredded napkins. She rose, motioning for him to follow. "In my office are some of the reasons. A picture's worth a thousand words. I could use a drink, as well. How about you?"

"Water, please."

Five minutes later, Bunny pulled two photos from the wall. She pushed them across her desk. Brent sat on the desk and pulled them closer. She uncapped her bottle and drank.

The first photo showed her and Derrick holding Christie as a toddler. She was pregnant with Phillip at the time it was taken. The second photo was of her mom.

Bunny smiled as she caught him scrutinizing her. "This is my mom." She tapped the frame closest to Brent. "She married late in life. My sister and I were miracles to her. She thought she'd never have kids. Dad married her despite that. They loved us and each other a lot."

She paused, swallowing hard. Some of the pain of loss had lessened over the years. The acute ache of emptiness and surrounding sorrow remained raw as if it were a near past occurrence. Taking a deep breath, she continued. "The other picture is me and my late husband."

Brent's eyes snapped to hers. "Late husband?" The curiosity tingeing his voice told her he didn't know or knew very little.

"Derrick and I were high school and college sweethearts." Tears salted her eyes. "We wed not long after his graduation from fire school." She traced the edges of the frame. Her fingers paused near Derrick's image. "Being an EMT wasn't enough." Tears flowed down her cheeks.

Brent pushed a crumpled napkin into her hand. "I didn't know," he muttered, his voice low and flat. "You don't—"

"Yes, I do. I can't hide any longer. It's time I stopped lying to myself."

She squeezed Brent's arm. Licking her lips, she continued. "Derrick wanted to be on the front lines. As Christy and Phillip, my eldest two, came along, he advanced, moving us around. Mom came along after Dad's death."

She heard Brent uncap his water as she wiped her eyes.

"He was an EMT-certified fireman." Brent's statement indicated he understood. His next said he followed where she led. "Like I am."

"I was pregnant with Kate when we decided to buy in Richmond. Mom settled into a retirement community not far from us. As Assistant Lead EMT, Derrick got a lot calls for the facility. One night, a fire broke out. Derrick responded as he was on call. He didn't see Mom in the crowd. He donned an oxygen tank and entered the building. Moments later, the roof collapsed and an explosion happened. They never made it out."

Heart-wrenching sobs racked her chest. Tears blurred her vision. "I fled as far as I could. I've been here since."

Two strong arms lifted her up. She struggled, pushing away. "I don't want your pity."

* * * *

"Shh," his voice whispered. "Let me hold you. Just hold you."

Settling her on his lap, he wrapped his arms around her and rocked them both. Her eyes darted away from his. His ex-wife played the come-hither game for two years, two long, frustrating years of waiting. She'd given physical satisfaction but withheld emotionally. He'd been too young to know. It wasn't until he caught her cheating that she finally confessed. She'd married him thinking he'd go into his brother's business. *Gold-digger*, she'd been after what she thought was his money or might eventually become his. Divorce had felt good and cleansing and yet was a hard lesson learned. His own tears leaked out his eyes. His heart ached for them both. Confession was good for the soul. He was next.

"I-I-I," he began, trying to find the words to explain why he cried with her. He paused, inhaling. Easing her off his lap, he kept her close.

"I know how it is to lose someone close to you in an instant. I was on duty on Nine-Eleven, commanding the station since my commander, captain, and several on duty responded with another battalion as the calls went out for backup. Only a few made it out or came back. Many were like family."

Bunny's arms slid around him as she scooted closer. Her sobs and sniffles reignited his own. Hugging her tighter, he closed his eyes and silently wept.

* * * *

Bunny looked out the window of the small plane—no, private jet—and reminded herself to breathe. She rolled her thoughts back to two weeks prior.

She wondered why she'd said yes. Yes to Brent's gift and a trip to New York. How far was she willing to go? And for what? She'd said yes even though her heart and gut said no.

Brent's confessed age of forty-two had caught her by surprise. His actions and manners were on par with hers. She'd estimated his age equal to hers. Though his boyish looks and youthful zeal made her subtract several years off how old she thought he was, four years wasn't a huge difference.

Brent's hand covered hers. He leaned over and kissed her cheek.

"Enjoying the view?" he whispered against her ear. His hot breath seared her sensitive earlobe, sending tendrils of desire to the right places. "I believe so," he added and nipped her earlobe.

Bunny fidgeted. Her mind raced for a reason to tell him to stop. No prying eyes were possible with the cockpit door securely closed.

No one else occupied the cabin. Her lids grew heavier as desire enveloped her in her own growing need. Her eyes closed at last. Reaching between them, she lifted the armrest and nestled closer. She heard and felt his sharp intake as she settled tighter against him.

His hands cupped her breasts. Heat shot through her. She could feel her nipples pebbling against his palms. One hand slid lower, rubbing along her ribcage. A soft, heated sigh warmed her cheek and ear. "*I* like the view."

Her eyes shot open. She worked to turn. He held her fast.

"Don't think. Just feel."

Her throat grew dryer, and her hormones refused to cool down. His hot words rasped close to her ear. Lips and teeth worried the delicate flesh between her ear and jaw. Each time he nipped, his fingers traced the outer edge of her hard nipple through her blouse. Lace chafed and teased her sensitive tip. Need coursed lower in her body. She watched his seeking fingers edge inside her blouse. He undid one, then two buttons, allowing his hand entrance. She gasped at his warm palm cupping and rubbing her jittery stomach. It worked higher.

He undid two more buttons. Her blouse parted, revealing her pale peach, lace demi bra. She'd heard about watching yourself in a mirror during sex. This was better. Her breasts slightly overflowed his hands. She'd palmed and plumped while getting dressed. It was never like this.

Her neck arched. She lay fully against him. Her eyes closed. He flicked his thumbs over her nipples in rapid succession. It was as if he kept time with her breathing.

"So beautiful," filled her ear. His tongue swirled and traced the whorls of her ear. He dropped lower, moving his lips from her lobe to her jaw. Lord, the man set her on fire. He worked lower, blowing back and forth over his marked path. She jumped as he bit. Leaning fuller in to him, she gave into her mounting desire. "Brent, it feels wonderful."

"Good." His muffled voice came from near the base of her throat. As his head moved lower, his hands moved higher, cupping her more. Soft moans escaped her tight lips.

"Twenty minutes till landing, sir."

Brent turned Bunny. "Sweetie, time to simmer for a while," he began, pulling her blouse back together. "I'll take a rain check until later, okay?" He helped her fasten the last few buttons. Bunny's soft sigh and whispered "yes" seemed to make his hands shake.

Chapter Six

Brent had forgotten what intermission at a Broadway play could be like. The throng of people milling about filled the lobby beyond comfortable capacity. As he scanned the crowd, watching for Bunny, he noted each exit along with the fire alarm and extinguisher locations. He might be off the clock, but he was never completely off duty.

It'd taken some talking and sharing on both their parts to get this far. He hoped the outcome was worth it. Bunny smiled as she approached.

Her dress hugged her in all the right places. His view took in her long, lean legs. Maybe later on tonight, they'd have him locked in their passionate embrace. Taking a deep breath, he moved his eyes upwards. He didn't need evidence of his thoughts sticking out.

Brent guided Bunny back to their seats and settled back with his arm draped across her shoulders, ready for the second half to begin. He hoped she would like the additional gift he'd arranged for her after the play.

* * * *

"Brent, thank you for a lovely evening." Bunny sighed, snuggling closer under the blanket covering them. Her delighted smile and eager nod when he proposed the carriage ride confirmed he'd made a good choice.

He watched the familiar skyline and sights pass by. He pointed out sections of Central Park filled with childhood memories. As they neared the fallen firefighters' memorial, he grew quiet. Every time he saw it, he couldn't hold in the emotion that threatened to swallow him.

* * * *

His hands grew cold and clammy. Bunny noticed the change. "Brent, what's wrong?"

She chafed his hand between hers. Drawing the blanket higher, she turned, following his gaze. The monument hit close to home for both of them. Streetlights illuminated his silent tears. She swallowed her own and stroked his cheek. It was her turn to be there for him, to urge him to share and let go.

"It's not easy losing someone you care about. It's even harder when it's several." She wondered how bad his ghosts were. He'd shared a bit the night they talked.

She heard his watery sigh. Closing her eyes, she prayed for guidance. She remembered her grief counselor's continued admonishment. *Talk about it. Keeping it bottled up prolongs the agony and delays healing.*

"Care to share?" she offered, knowing a forced discussion wasn't a good option. Brent's soft "no" kept her from probing further.

"J-just," his voice faded to a whisper, "just hold me."

She urged his head to her shoulder and tightly wrapped her arms around him. A shooting star flashed across the dark sky, and she remembered one of Derrick's strong-held beliefs. *Each time a star shoots across the sky, angels are sending a message.* Maybe the message was that there was a reason they were together.

* * * *

Brent remained quiet the remainder of the ride to the hotel. His composure regained, he waited until they reached the suite to delve into the subject further.

"Thanks for being there for me. I didn't realize how raw my own memories are." He tossed his suit coat on the sofa and sat, running his hands through his hair.

Bunny sat beside him. She pulled his hand into hers. "I sense there's more. I'm listening."

"You know about Marta, my ex."

Bunny nodded.

"A few years after our divorce, she came to me asking for help locating work. We'd mended our fences over the marriage. She'd fallen on hard times and needed a job. Between Randy and me, we got her several connections. She placed with a firm on the twenty-second floor of one of the World Trade Center towers. She'd gone in early the morning of September eleventh. I'd dropped her off as her car was in the shop. She never made it out."

His ragged sigh filled the room. "We argued as usual, and she refused to let me help her any more. I still cared. More than I knew. Two of my best friends were on the responding squads. One radioed my station saying he was watching for her. Neither of them made it out as the second tower collapsed. My captain ordered me to stay behind to man the remaining engine crew."

"You ran from your pain like me," Bunny said quietly.

Brent nodded, starring at the carpet and his feet. "In a way, yes." He bounced his folded hands between his legs. Raising his head, he looked her straight in the eye. "Guilt and remorse consumed me. I did nothing and couldn't. I felt helpless as I watched the unfolding drama on television over and over. I was diagnosed with post-traumatic stress and put on disability furlough for six months." He paused, waiting and watching Bunny's reaction.

Bunny cupped his chin, angling his face. She stroked his cheek, leaning closer. He could see the concern and care filling her eyes. She hadn't flinched or turned away. "It's never easy." She brushed her lips over his.

"It was like a double sentence. Not being able to help and being told you're not capable of helping." Bunny looped her arm over his shoulders and squeezed.

"Yes." Brent let out a deep breath. "I'd come up for promotion shortly before Nine-Eleven. I got offered captain, though I tested and placed for chief. My therapist suggested a change of scenery might help. I couldn't remain idle. I took the promotion and returned to work. Rotating stations and sections of town every couple of years didn't dull the memories and pain as much as I thought it would. Distance seemed the best option. I applied and took my current job."

* * * *

Bunny stood and pulled him with her. Running her hands halfway up his arms, she stepped closer. She toed off her shoes, kicking them aside.

"Life hasn't been easy for either of us. You moved and continued living, doing your job, and healing. Me, I ran and put myself on autopilot for the sake of the kids and what I thought I was dealing with." She circled her arms around Brent's neck.

"I hid from the pain and a lot of unresolved feelings. I'm glad we found each other," he replied, placing his hands on her hips.

Threading her hands into his hair, she tugged him to her. "Kiss my pain away as I do yours," she murmured huskily.

Brent's hand moved to her waist. He fumbled with her belt as he stepped closer. The sound of it hitting the carpet followed. "Too many constraints can hamper the healing process."

"I agree." She worked his tie free, flinging it over her shoulder. Hip to hip they stood, their mutual breaths heating their glowing embers of desire. Her eyes fluttered closed as his lips neared hers.

Light flashed behind her eyelids. Heat worked its way down her stomach, sinking lower, pooling between her legs. Flames rushed toward her middle.

The first brush of his lips primed her growing need. Memories of their earlier kisses flooded her subconscious desire. Parting her lips, she granted him entrance. Her tongue met his.

Brent pushed closer. Stroking his thigh against hers, he urged her legs apart. He rode her, mimicking his primal want. Her soft "mmm" allowed him to deepen their kiss. Running his hands to her buttocks, he held her tight, rubbing his hardness against her as intimately as he could.

The heat between them grew, each seeking solace and healing. Brent wanted more. He needed to know there was something beyond now. A spontaneous act would quench momentary needs, but he was ready for more. What did more look like? He didn't know. He'd told Bunny not to think, just feel. Maybe it was time to take his own advice.

Bunny dragged her nails gently along his scalp. Massaging her hands firmly back and forth over his head and neck, he felt the tension ebbing. Breaking off their kiss, he breathlessly whispered, "That feels great."

Resting her forehead on his, Bunny blinked. Brent's gorgeous brown eyes met hers. Warmth and passion greeted her. Her own reflection vividly colored by his view fueled her growing need. She dropped her hands to his shoulders.

Well-defined muscles rippled and corded under her seeking fingers. His shirt bunched and moved as her hands gripped and soothed. Memories of doing the same to Derrick flooded through her. She hesitated, waiting for the pain and agony to begin. It didn't. Care and genuine concern grew. Perhaps Brent might like a back rub.

"Why don't we get comfortable?" She knew she was taking a risk asking.

She ached to massage the warm, masculine flesh and felt it beneath her oiled hands. A need to nurture and connect throbbed deep in her belly. Moving her hands to his chest, she sprawled them close to the middle buttons.

Brent's hands covered hers. "Are you sure?" His hot breath caressed her cheek. His eyes never wavered from hers.

"Yes." Her hands slid from his. One step back and she fingered open two buttons. Dark brown chest hair peeked through. Gone was the regulation white T-shirt. Her fingers twitched, itching to touch what lay before her. One stroke—just one—to feed her yearning need to connect and know someone else was there.

Brent pulled his shirt free of his waistband. Shaking it out, he loosened another button. Her throat went dry. Heat rushed north and south. Her breasts grew heavy with need and her panties dewier. She'd seen him shirtless before but not this close up and personal. Touching and tasting were permissible. God, she hoped they were. Her fingers grazed the open v.

"Turn around." His low, whispered command caught her off guard. "My turn to assist the lady." His hands reached for the back of her dress. A short zipper and hook-n-eye held it in place on her shoulders. Once undone, the straps would slide lower. She was glad she'd chosen the bra and panties she had.

Bunny turned, stepping over her shoes and away from Brent. She held out her hand. "A bit more room might help." Presenting her back, she added, "I believe you asked for this."

* * * *

Brent moved around the coffee table and stopped a hair's breadth from her. Her shapely buttocks and hips framed by her dress drew his gaze. Each time she raised her arms, the dress tightened and accentuated the area. His cock grew harder. Images of her nude and on her hands and knees revved his hormones into high gear.

He'd fumbled earlier, working the delicate fastener closed with his large fingers. Hoping it cooperated this time, he focused. Slender, graceful fingers came into view. They swiftly undid the hook-n- eye. He caught her wink as her hands dropped back to her sides.

Several strands of hair fell out of her clip and wispy curls brushed her shoulders. He swallowed and counted. Softness and femininity combined with strength and perseverance. She intrigued him, unlike anyone else had since Marta.

Grasping the zipper tab, he eased it downward. Copper material parted, revealing lightly tanned skin. He edged it lower. Peach lace peeked out. Brent swallowed, working his dry throat. Her shoulders hunched and rolled back toward him. Copper shimmered down her arms. His arms sank to her waist and pulled her back to him.

Her buttocks pillowed against his growing hardness. He sucked in his stomach and tightened his ass cheeks, hoping to create some space between their lower heat levels. Her quiet *oh* said he'd succeeded in pressing himself firmer against her.

He rubbed in widening circles closer to her breasts. She leaned back into him. Her head rested on his chest. Her bared neck teased and taunted him. Unable to resist, he lowered his head and nibbled.

Various sexual poses raced through his mind. Between her verbalized pleasure and her touch, he wouldn't last much longer. He nipped her ear and asked, "Shall I stop?"

* * * *

Shivers ran down her back, rippling her growing pool of desire. Leaning forward, she shook her head. "No, don't stop." She paused, waiting to see if Brent moved with her. He remained still. Turning carefully to not move her dress further, she faced him. "I don't want you to stop."

She stroked his cheek. His watchful gaze showed his doubt. Pulling his hand from her waist, she grasped it firmly.

"I don't want to stop." She added, "I'm sure," at his continued quietness.

Doubt crept into her thoughts. Had she said or done something wrong? Why was he quiet?

"What's wrong?" she asked, releasing his hand.

Brent cleared his throat. "Nothing. I'm working on not ravishing you and yet asking why now and not before."

Relief washed over her as he spoke. He wanted it all to make sense. Tonight was for feeling. She'd deal with repercussions in the morning.

She needed to reconnect with the lost side of herself, glorify in her femininity, and enjoy passionate lust without issue and baggage. Could Brent?

He opened his mouth to speak. She placed her fingers over it. "Shh," she quietly began, "Just feel. Be in the moment with me. It feels right. The trust is right. This is our oasis, our time of healing. Tomorrow is soon enough for why. *Please.*"

Brent nodded, offering his outstretched hand. She grasped it. He pulled her to him. His rapid tug sent her stumbling against him. He swept her up in his arms, settling her close to his chest. The steady thrum of his heart filled her ear as he entered the suite's bedroom.

* * * *

Her body hotly slid down his. Brent carefully set Bunny on her feet. He brushed his lips over hers. He turned, dimming the glaring overhead light to a soft glow. Low-volume classical music played in the background, shutting out the noise of the city. He pulled his belt from his pants, draping it on the doorknob. His cuff links tumbled on the bedside table. Rolling up his sleeves, he faced her. His arms outstretched, he spoke, "Welcome to our cocoon of healing." He crooked his finger in a come-hither motion.

Placing her hand over her heart, she walked towards him. Copper slipped down one arm, freeing it, then the other. Light tan decorated with peach, lace-covered straps graced her shoulders. The color almost matched her nails. He made a mental note of her color preference. His male ego, horny with need, teased him with taunts of what about black lace lingerie. Another time, another place, perhaps. Not tonight. Tonight was about here and now.

She stopped and dropped her hands. Copper shimmered down, catching on her hips on its decent, pooling at her feet. His breathing turned shallow. His throat constricted. Panties matching their counterpart greeted his eyes. To hell with black lace, *hello* peach.

Bikini cut panties adorned her full, womanly hips. Trimmed pubic hair shadowed the region between her legs. She had legs that wouldn't quit, muscled and toned in all the right places. Dryness gripped his throat and mouth. What would those legs feel like wrapped around his waist? Flung over his shoulder as he tasted and pleasured her orally? She drew closer, her dress draped over her arm.

"Penny for your thoughts." Her husky tone made his stomach clutch. Could she know his thoughts? He gulped, reminding himself to breathe. Did she know the effect she had on him? Her low laugh and soft smile pulled him out of himself.

"Ah umm," he stammered, searching for words. If he wasn't careful, he'd blurt out his crass thoughts.

* * * *

She tittered, passing him. She hung her dress in her clothes carrier. Bunny wondered how vulnerable she dared being. She knew she trusted Brent to not hurt or harm her. Anxiety leveled to negligible when he'd sat the box of condoms on the nightstand. She liked his upfront preparedness. Life was too short to not be lived. Was she ready to start believing them and living by them? Use them for herself instead of everyone else?

A cool tendril whipped down her spine and rumbled deep in her psyche. How many times had she mouthed those words? Used them in advising friends, family, and her children? *Just feel, think tomorrow* echoed through her soul. Taking a deep breath, she flattened herself against his back, wrapping her arms around his waist.

Her hands moved lower. Reaching his zippered fly, she nipped his ear.

"Dare you to share." Her tongue laved his earlobe.

"Share what?" he asked, turning to embrace her.

"Your innermost thoughts. I dare each of us to speak our mind. Reveal our needs, wants, and desires of this moment. Risk being vulnerable."

Silence hung between them. She didn't break his stare. It was as if each waited for the other to move or speak first. Blasts of cold air pelted them. Looking up, they began laughing together. In the ceiling above them was the central air vent.

She chafed her arms, moving sideways. "This might help." Brent wrapped his shirt around her.

Bare-chested, he stood still. Bunny pulled his shirt tightly around her. She bolted to the bed. Pulling back the covers, she jumped in. Blankets secure around her, she held out Brent's shirt, dropping it on the floor. Her eyes followed his hands.

He unbuttoned his waistband. He eased his trousers lower until they caught on his hips. His hand moved down, tracing his tented crotch. Slowly working his zipper open, he approached the bed. With each step, his trousers exposed more. Another blast of cold air billowed out the vent.

"So much for a seductive strip," he spit out, teeth chattering as he joined Bunny.

Snickers and giggles erupted from her. His shirt and pants lay abandoned on the floor. "Come here and warm me." He tugged at the blankets and sheets. She shook her head, clasping the covers tighter.

"No, you warm me." He slid across the bed, grabbing her and the blankets, too. He rolled her beneath him.

He pulled the layers from between them. Cool limbs entwined her warmer ones. Her short-lived eeks and muffled squeals peppered the air. "Ah, warmth." His satisfied tone made her grin.

He rocked against her, his arousal apparent. Warmth replaced their earlier chill.

She licked her lips. Rolling to his side, he took her with him. His lips touched hers. Her muffled, "Haven't we done this before?" went unanswered.

Her open mouth gained him entrance. Her tongue met and entwined his. Nudging her legs apart, he wedged his knee and thigh between them. He rocked her tighter to him. One hand slid down her hip, pulling her panties lower. She did the same with his briefs. Combined body movements rubbed silk and lace together, adding to their heightened frenzy.

* * * *

Breathless, Bunny broke the kiss. Sucking in air, she held her breath, willing her heart to slow. Brent didn't. His hand traced and skimmed in a feather-light pendulum motion, caressing her exposed flesh from the edge of her bra to mid hip. His other hand plucked and pulled her remaining hairpins free. Her hair fell to her shoulders.

She gasped as he rocked her hard against him. His hand tangled in her hair and held her tight. A muffled swat followed as his hand connected with her ass. She squirmed at his heated breath pouring over her nipples. He suckled, taking her lace-covered tip deep in his mouth.

Wetness engulfed her sensitive peak. Her engorged nipples chafed against the lace, wringing trails of need deeper and hotter into her heightened arousal. Brent's palm flowed over her shoulder, toying with her bra strap. Working it downward, he stopped. Her eyes fluttered open. He grinned.

"I want to bury myself deep inside you. Your pleasure is important to me, too."

Disengaging himself, he sat up. Blankets and sheets pooled at his waist. He scooted to the bed's edge. Getting Bunny's attention, he removed his watch, placing it next to his cuff links. "No need to repeat that." His saucy wink warmed her, growing more heat. He tossed aside the covers and stood. He hooked his thumbs into his silk briefs and shoved them down his hips.

Bunny tried to swallow. Show and look had begun. Her gaze darted to his. Calm passion flared, darkening his eyes. Brent bent and retrieved his briefs. How could the man know the view of his tight, firm ass and dangling balls drenched her wet panties even more? Pictures of his contracting ass cheeks as he pumped in and out of her flooded her mind. Okay, so she was a sucker for mirrored ceilings.

His cock, hardening and thickening more, rose as she looked. Her nipples grew harder and throbbed. His endowment, a bit more than average, made her mouth and panties wetter. She enjoyed oral sex and being filled full. Would he think her forward and be turned off like Derrick had?

* * * *

Brent laid his briefs near his shirt and trousers. He could feel her giving him the once-over. If they were to get any further, he needed and wanted her trust. Would she be willing to give it?

He slid beneath the covers and settled next to her. Hooking his finger in her bra strap, he tugged it off her shoulder. "I think one of us is a bit overdressed."

His fingers traced the top of her bra, lingering as they met at the dip of her cleavage. "I can help," he suggested.

Bunny shook her head. She wet her lips and moved from the bed. Her turn had come. Brent could tell by the quick look of panic that crossed her face that she was afraid. Did she fear undressing or something else?

He relaxed in hopes of calming her. He wanted her to know he was interested but didn't want to scare her. He pushed the covers to his knees. His fingers encircled his cock, and he stroked downward.

She slowly relaxed and let her bra float down, landing on the bed. She cupped her breasts, and his cock jerked. She smiled, and he stroked faster. Skimming her panties off, she bared all before him. He ached with need and was sure it showed on his face.

Chapter Seven

Outside their high-rise oasis, thunder boomed, echoing off the surrounding lower buildings. Flashes of lightning sizzled through the air, growing in heat as hot and cold air currents undulated together. A loud roar shook several exteriors. Soft rain fell, cooling the parched cement and metal edifices. Inside, two lovers lay spooned together, watching nature's show.

Bunny snuggled deeper beneath the covers, seeking Brent's warmth. How long had it been since she'd sought out comfort and companionship like this? Too long, if she couldn't remember. A sense of ease filled her, and yet, she remained unsure if she dared acknowledge feeling.

Brent's arms captured her waist, pulling her closer. She went willingly. His chin rested a top her head. His slow, steady breathing relaxed her yearning hormones to a sedated level. Drawing a deep breath, she settled her hips against his. She sensed his unspoken, ravenous want hovering at the edge of his control. It puzzled her.

She'd dared them to speak their truths and be vulnerable. They'd shed their outer trappings and revealed their physical bareness. Had time come for the mental aspect? His deep sigh prevented further speculation.

"Why the sigh?" she asked. Anxiety dripped its ice-cold venom close to her heart. Was he rejecting her? She chewed her lip, awaiting his response.

* * * *

Brent heaved another deep-cleansing sigh. He longed for moments of peaceful quiet time shared with someone he cared for. Need ached deep in his groin. He'd act upon it soon enough. He wanted no regrets come morning. He knew tonight marked a beginning. One he didn't plan on ending.

"Contentment, my dear. Contentment." He felt her pull away. His closed eyes snapped open. She turned to face him, remaining close.

"What do you mean?" Her uneasy tone clued him to the reason she asked. He cupped her face and brushed his lips over hers.

"Marta and most other women I've dated didn't understand the quiet reassuring need of touch. Just holding someone and being together, relaxed and at ease." He smiled at her understanding nod.

"I want you. Not at the expense of a quick lay." Her fingers on his lips stilled his further words. He pushed them aside and pressed his lips to hers.

His hope turned a bit sour at her reminder to be in the moment. His heart beat loudly, drumming its message of patience and waiting. All was not as it appeared. Healing took time. Better to allow trust to grow and gain mutual acceptance. She'd revealed a lot in the last few days. He remembered his own torn, ragged feelings learning to date again. It had been a hard journey to trust himself once more.

Time was for now. Enjoy the moment and worry about tomorrow tomorrow. Words he'd eagerly embraced during his furlough. His obstinate male self-image and warring heart softened their uproar.

Wrapping his arms around her, he rolled her on her back. Her startled surprise parted her lips from his.

Pubic hair rubbed over his hips as he settled between her legs. Her heated, dewy petals pushed open, cradling his eight-inch hardness. Supporting his weight on his forearms, he circled his hips on and over her. Pre-cum rolled down his cock head, mixing with her wetness, lubricating their heated contact.

"Oh God," escaped Bunny's lips. Her eyes, dark with passion, met his. He pressed heavier and closer. He slid his cock slid over her taut clit. He felt her rippled response. Rising up on his hands, he enjoyed the view. He bet her engorged nipples were as sensitive as her swollen clit.

"Place your hands above your head," he whispered against her ear as he lowered his chest to hers.

She hesitated. She furled her brow. "Huh?" Her reply was muffled by his shoulder.

"Place your hands above your head. I don't want to lay on them."

* * * *

Her rational side demanded to know why, and yet her heart echoed *trust him*. She'd come this far. A bit further wouldn't hurt. Would it?

Her hands over her head, she gasped. His teeth found the sensitive spot between her jaw and ear. His hand traced the same relative area on the opposite side. Spirals of desire wove their intricate lattice around her aching peaks of desire, twisting and turning her raging hormones into an inferno.

Her hips rocked toward his. He blew on the wet trail leading lower. Would he ever reach her nipples? Her clit thrummed, and her nipples echoed their reply with each pulse of her heart.

"B-Brent."

Her voice broke. Arching her back, she pushed against his wet, heated tongue flicking over and around first one nipple then the other. He rolled and tweaked her abandoned nipple between his thumb and finger. His lips moved lower. The assault stopped.

She lay panting, working labored breaths in and out her nose rather than her open mouth. Her fragmented sense-of-being refused to cohere. Parts of her tingled, crying out for more. Lord, she wanted whatever he was dishing out. Had she gone over the edge? Surrendered her control?

Memories of her last few relationships lingered more than she cared. Panic threatened to overflow its small puddle at the back of her mind. He hadn't done anything unusual or susceptible. She'd come this far, and she wasn't turning back.

"Hmmm" spilled out of her partly closed mouth. He twisted and turned her captured nipples like two screws between his thumb and forefinger. His wet nips and licks trailed toward her waist. *God*, the man had her tottering on the precipice of need, urging her higher, back into the clouded peaks of surrender.

* * * *

Raising his head, Brent admired his handiwork. He grinned, watching Bunny squirm as he tweaked her nipples harder. Returning to his path, he blew over her navel, grinning more when she sucked it in. Did she think she'd escape his hungry descent?

The tip of his tongue, barely past his teeth and lips, dragged along the hollow beginning below her navel and moved lower. Strands of pubic hair tickled his chin. He nibbled back and forth, up and down, leaving no area untouched above her pubis.

Trailing his fingertips lightly, he traced the undersides of her breasts, marveling at their fullness and the firm muscles. His cock throbbed against his belly. His balls hung hot and eager for release. Lifting his hips, he moved lower on the bed. His hands caressed the outer fringes of her dewy petals. Her swollen nether lips barely covered her glistening, erect clit. He licked his lips in anticipation.

Bunny clutched the pillows supporting her. Brent feathered his fingertip closer to her clit. Snaking his hand under each thigh, he raised her. It was as if she helped, jerking her hips forward. Was she saying yes? He'd soon find out.

Brent placed her legs over his shoulders. Wrapping his arms around her hips, he peeled her open. Moist, pink flesh topped with her taut clit greeted him. He inhaled her womanly fragrance. Marked with her scent, he blew gently along her dampness. Her vocal responses ramped up his desire several degrees higher.

Bunny combed his head and hair with her hands. Unable to resist the morsel in front of him, Brent suckled her clit between his puckered lips. He held her fast. Her hips pressed higher and tighter to him with each lick.

Her short, breathy pants reached his ears. Her deep-throated sighs and moans increased. She held him firm as she thrust and ground against his growing assault. Flicking his tongue in short, rapid strokes, Brent loosened his grip on her hips. He coated two fingers with her wetness and outlined her vagina. On her next thrust, he pressed his fingers in.

She flexed and tightened around his seeking fingers. Lord, how long had it been since he'd watched a woman react to his touch? Her soft flesh and deep sighs tugged at part of him he'd forgotten about. He took great pride and satisfaction in pleasure well done and thoroughly *enjoyed*.

* * * *

She groaned and raised her hips, shaking each time he fondled the flesh nearest his middle finger. He found her g-spot and rubbed more.

Joy boiled deep inside her. Bunny gasped and hummed. Catching her bottom lip between her teeth, she worried it softly. So close and yet not quite enough, she cried out, asking for and wanting more. Wave upon wave of pleasure washed over her, taking her off her precipice higher onto richer, stronger orgasms. Her core pitched and tossed her heavenward. Orgasmic bliss flooded over, through and around her.

She counted to ten and opened her eyes. Damn, the man was good. No wonder Amy had fussed about sex curing what ailed you. As she looked at him, her heart melted a little. No one had cared about her pleasure and participation before. Whether she cared to admit it or not, she was glad she'd pushed her boundaries and come to New York with Brent.

He lay on his side, grinning. Sparks of satisfaction smirked across his face. He almost glowed in an egotistical way. His gaze and upturned mouth drew her focus. Taking a deep breath, she faced him. A flash of silver caught her focus.

A foil packet dangled between Brent's fingers. He dropped the condom between them. Bunny glanced down to where it lay. Was he silently challenging her? Or letting her decide where they went next?

"I put my pleasure in your hands." Brent took her hand, placing it on his cock. His pre-cum lubricated her fingers as he slid back and forth between them. He rimmed a finger around his cock head and turned to her. Tracing her lips, he glossed them with his juices. "Or in your hot mouth," he huskily added, drawing his finger slowly in and out of her pursued lips.

Bunny worked her throat, trying to find her voice much less swallow. The man knew what buttons to push. Maybe she shouldn't have dared him. *Sister, you've got to be kidding,* her psyche bellowed. *The man is offering you the chance for no-holds-barred sex, and you're laying here, trying to rationalize it? Honey, enjoy! Or maybe you care more than you'd like to admit?*

"Cock got your tongue?" Brent teased, winking at her as he laid back.

Bunny picked up the condom packet. Meeting Brent's gaze was out of the question. The man was reading her too damn well. She roved her focus lower and ordered her gaze to stop at his waist. Curiosity won, drawing her straight to his crotch.

Eight beautiful inches greeted her. Firm, eager for action, it stood stiff, jetting out from his pubic hair. Wet droplets glistened along its top. She couldn't help herself, or could she? Licking her lips in anticipation, she scooted closer.

Carefully, she enclosed her hand around him. Brent's hissed *yes* told her she was doing something right. She stroked up and over him, rubbing her palm lightly over his tip, moistening her fingers. Moving in an unsteady rhythm, she stroked him base to tip, once, twice, until his hand covered hers.

"Much more and I'll come. Unless that's your preference. I'd rather it be your mouth or inside you." Brent's tight-lipped look and clenched hand backed up his words.

Bunny glanced at her full hand. His tip poked out at the top, she could taste him unabashed. No worries or extra precautions. "A small taste, sir, if you please."

Leaning forward, she slid her hand to his base and lower, fondling his balls. She cupped them and softly kneaded. Pants and hisses spurred her next move.

Bringing her palm back to his base, she held him firm. With her free hand, she used her teeth to tear open the foil packet. Palming the condom, she made her decision.

Dropping her head, she licked. A salty, masculine flavor exploded across her taste buds. Brent's hips jerked as her mouth engulfed him. Duplicating his assault to her clit, she laved and suckled him. His fingers tangled in her hair, guiding her. After a quick slurp down and back, she released him. Using the hand holding him, she continued caressing.

Placing the condom inside her mouth, she engulfed him again. Tonguing him tip to base, she mouthed the condom over him. Rocking back, she waited, admiring her effect.

Brent's chest rose in labored, ragged breaths. He gripped the strewn blankets and sheets. His passionate dark eyes met hers. Not one to leave a task unfinished, Bunny met their unspoken challenge.

Straddling Brent, she guided him deep within. She was full. Her hands splayed on his chest, she rose to the point of almost losing him. He grasped her waist. "Slow and steady, love. I like to savor my main courses."

His illicit groan as she sank back on him struck a spark within her. *Slow and steady wins the race* ran through her mind. Why was she racing? They had all night. *Or the rest of our lives?*

Bunny gulped hard. Where had that come from? Panic reared its ugly, unwelcomed head, demanding its sacrifice. With none offered, it claimed its victim—her sense of wellbeing.

* * * *

Lying deep within her, Brent felt Bunny's emotional shudder. Her tear-sparkled eyes signaled her silent despair. "Stop?" he offered, thumbing a stray tear from her cheek.

"No," her voice broke, "the past seeks to break our peace." She rocked her hips, clutching him in place.

Pulling her to him, he guided their rhythm, increasing the pressure and pace until culmination embraced them once again.

* * * *

Brent stared at the key filling his hand. The six weeks it had taken to bring the house up to code and finish readying it for his move-in had flown by. He looked up.

"Something wrong, Brent?" Marie Foster's voice cut through his wanderlust musings.

"No. It's a bit surreal to finally have the keys to *my* home." He inserted the key bearing a large F into the lock. Hearing it open, Brent raised his eyes skyward. Mouthing a silent *thank you*, he pushed open the dark teak wood door. He was home even if his stuff wasn't.

The open floor plan enhanced the grace of the older home. Off the paneled entryway, the pale celery-green living room walls reflected natural light from the large floor to ceiling windows. What would Bunny think? He followed Marie into the combined kitchen and dining area.

Vibrant golden yellow accents framed the hunter green walls. Mosaic tiles in varying hues matching the wall color created the stove and sink back splashes. New stainless steel appliances dotted the far wall. Brent smiled at the dishwasher. He remembered Bunny's passing remark about doing dishes by hand while she waited for the café's replacement.

Marie turned to head upstairs. Brent hesitated. Only a few minutes in the house, and he'd thought of Bunny twice. Man, he had it bad.

"Everything okay?" Marie's question jerked him back.

"Umm...yes." She cast him a surprised look. "Sorry, Marie, I got caught up in daydreaming. Planning, you know." Her smile said she bought his line. Damn, he needed to keep his wits about him.

Brent followed her, lost in his musings. Bunny claimed more and more of his thoughts. Last time he'd been this bad, it'd been Marta. *Crap!* He ran full force into Marie. She stumbled, catching herself on the banister.

"Sorry, Marie." He forced a chuckle, hoping it matched his sheepish grin. Out of the corner of his eye, he saw the reason for her pause.

Two-tone walls, beige and ecru, split in the middle with blue chair-rail molding, decorated his stairwell. He didn't remember this combination. It was Marie's turn to grin and shrug.

"Is the rest as bad?" Where had his head been when he made these decisions?

"I'll let you decide." Marie's flat tone didn't sound good. He walked partway down the hall. The guest bath, done up in two-tone pale beiges and browns, appeared fine. Across from it sat two smaller bedrooms. The first, his planned den, displayed warm, rich hues of marine blue and white. The other room echoed the living room's color with pale red accents. Brent shrugged. As a guest room, it wouldn't see much use.

He faced the last doors in the hall. Double, dark wood doors graced the opening. His master bedroom. Strong, rich earth tones, muted browns, and greens with touches of ochre welcomed him. He pictured his furniture placed and ready around the room. Somehow, it didn't feel right. "Oh shit," he muttered. Had he gotten so use to pink walls and Bunny, he'd be uncomfortable in his own place?

He returned to Marie. "Some color choices I don't remember making." He chuckled. "Paint chips don't always match the end result."

Marie smiled, nodding. "Let's go back to my office. You can sign off on everything and move in."

Brent looked out across the open lower level as he descended the stairs. His furniture and possessions would soon occupy the space. He wanted more than a bachelor's place. He wanted a home, feminine touches included. Bunny's insight and choices would add what he was looking for.

Outside, he turned to lock the door. It hit him. He was already seeing Bunny with him as a couple. His hand shook as he locked the door. Fear rolled through his gut. Fear he'd taken on more than he was ready for. He needed to find out though if she was avoiding him. Was she running or hiding again?

Chapter Eight

Outside traffic and the jangle of the bell above the café door interrupted Bunny's train of thought. Looking up, expecting to see Brent, she frowned. It was Amy.

Bunny hadn't seen much of Amy since her return from her first-aid recertification classes the first two weeks of the month. The last two weeks, Amy had stopped by long enough to grab coffee and food to go. She'd been unusually quiet and refused to say more than she was busy working crazy hours. As much as Bunny wanted to question her and find out what was going on, she knew Amy would talk when she was ready. Bunny just wished it was sooner than later.

Amy removed her sunglasses. Her puckered brow and red eyes said something wasn't right.

"Ben, can you watch the front? Kate should be home shortly. She'll help you out."

Ben's short *yeah* barely reached her ears. She'd already rounded the counter and headed toward Amy.

"Hon, you look like hell! What's wrong?"

Amy's ragged sigh cut Bunny to the quick. Whatever it was, for Amy to be this shaken, meant it wasn't simple. Taking her arm, Bunny directed her to the office.

Inside, Bunny shut the door. Settling Amy in the closest chair, Bunny set a box of tissues between them on the desktop. "Breathe," she encouraged Amy.

Bunny pulled two bottles of water from the corner cooler. She pressed one into Amy's hand. "Drink, and then tell me what's wrong."

Bunny opened her bottle and drank. Last time she'd seen Amy this upset was at a family funeral. She hoped it wasn't that.

Amy sighed heavily. "Just call me stupid, and I'm gonna lose my job," she blurted out.

Bunny dropped into the chair facing Amy. "Lose your job? How?"

"You're gonna—"

Bunny covered Amy's hand with hers, stopping her.

"Just tell me what happened." She patted her hand. "Recriminations can wait."

"You know Brent went for continuing education to keep up his training instructor certification?"

Bunny sat back in her chair, swallowing fast. Had Brent mentioned this? It didn't help she'd been avoiding him except for limited direct contact. She'd asked for time to think. That had been two weeks ago. Terror licked its icy way into her stomach. Was today's training like Derrick's? He'd faced a blazing hot fire in simulation after simulation. He'd called his burn scars his honor badges. Had Brent experienced the same?

Taking a deep breath, Bunny sighed and closed her eyes. She worked to calm her jittery nerves. "Go on," she quietly urged.

Can I hear this? Be objective for Amy? Other thoughts rushed in, only to be silenced as Amy spoke.

"Brent and I partnered for an exercise." Amy paused. The look on Bunny's face said she didn't know what she was talking about. "Let me start over." She waited for Bunny's short nod before proceeding.

"Remember I mentioned having to attend some continuing ed classes as part of my first-aid recertification?"

"Yes. I agreed to pet-sit for you."

"What I didn't mention was Brent's connection or my testing for promotion."

* * * *

Amy drew her lips tight over her teeth. She worried the inner edges of each. Acid lapped up her throat to pool with other brackish tastes present. The fact that Bunny was quiet added fuel to the increased anxiety brewing in her stomach. She asked the silent question forming between them. "Why didn't I tell you, right?"

* * * *

Bunny capped her bottle, sitting it on her desk. She rose and perched on the corner nearest Amy. She counted to five and exhaled. Patting Amy's arm, she spoke.

"The thought flashed through my mind, yeah. I know you don't speak out of turn. You don't tell what isn't yours to say."

Bunny watched Amy slide back in her chair. Her hands continued to fidget with her empty bottle. Apparently, she had more to say. "Tell me what happened."

"Brent showed up as one of the instructors. A couple of the classes required partners. With only three women in the class and an odd number of men, Brent offered to be my partner."

"Okay."

"What I didn't know was he was going through instructor certification. One of the tests was a simulated rescue."

Bunny bit her lip and swallowed hard. Her fears were being confirmed. Vivid images of Derrick's bruised and splotchy burn marks resurrected. Chills ran over her arms. She motioned for Amy to continue.

"I had to follow Brent's instructions and rescue him while he talked me through it. Once he was safe, first aid was next. We were allowed two practice runs."

"And?" Bunny asked impatiently. Uncertainty and fear compounded her growing agitation.

"The run went fine. We worked on some communication issues and word fuzziness which led us to agree to try again. As required, we threaded the safety rope through the ladder rungs, and we secured it around both our waists. Both ends were fastened to winch on the truck." Amy sighed and squeezed Bunny's arm. "Everything was working according to plan until our training rope broke, and I stumbled coming off the last rung of the ladder. I had Brent over my shoulders in a fireman's carry. His weight shifted as I stumbled."

"Go on," Bunny prompted, wringing her hands together.

"Brent tried to catch himself and slid off my shoulder to his feet. Our combined momentum threw him off, landing us both on his ankle."

Catching her breath, Bunny clenched fists. "How bad is it?" she asked, peering through her lashes.

Amy's hesitations and second ragged sigh indicated it wasn't good. "Brent's ankle is broken in two places. He faces screws and surgery if it doesn't heal right."

Bunny unclenched her fists. He wasn't maimed or scarred. Broken bones healed. So far so good. Her tense muscles relaxed.

Amy's nervous cough and jittering stopped Bunny's musings. "Yes?" she asked, noticing the tears leaking down Amy's cheeks.

"His Achilles tendon is sprained, too. He kept worrying about me. I stood there slack-jawed for several moments before my training kicked in."

"Hon," Bunny began, rising off her desk, "you had no way of knowing the rope would break, causing Brent to slip. You did the best you could."

"Yes, but the issue is under review, and a full reprimand could come from it. Severe enough to terminate me." Amy's watery sob yanked Bunny's fair play button.

"Why would they do that?" The question spilled out before she realized she'd spoken aloud.

"Brent and Captain Standferd reassured me they didn't see it going that far, but they did counsel me on the policies and procedures."

"Well, hon, telling you not to worry is fruitless."

Amy chuckled, adding, "Yeah, a bit after the fact, wouldn't you say?"

Bunny smiled, opening her office door. Looking at the clock, she asked, "Aren't you on duty? It's early for lunch."

"Oh yeah, on duty. *Nursemaid* duty." Amy's forced grin made Bunny snort.

"Okay, I get the sarcasm. Explain."

"I'm on temporary assignment, pending the outcome of the investigation" Amy paused, shaking her head. Her gaze met Bunny's. "Let's say I'm getting to know my boss better than I *ever* expected." Amy folded her arms and stared at her.

Bunny pressed her lips together, trying not to laugh or smile. She felt for Amy. Yet, at the same time, both could be somewhat hardheaded.

"It's your fault, too, you know." Amy pointed at her as Bunny snickered.

"How so?' Bunny walked out of the office and faced Amy. "Seriously, please explain."

"If you hadn't been avoiding Brent, you'd know this and be taking care of him instead of me."

"Oh?"

"Yes. Least you could do is help. Brent sent me over here to get his lunch. Something about your meatloaf special."

Bunny nodded, glancing toward the kitchen. Ben made one mean meatloaf. Ex-military cook, Ben knew about spices and sauces enhancing flavor and taste. Combined with her upgrade from ground beef to ground chuck roast, meatloaf became Kater's Wednesday and Sunday dinner special. Tapping her chin, she grinned.

"Tell you what. You let Brent know you've arranged delivery of his meals for the next couple of days. You could use a few hours to yourself. Go home and relax. I'll handle our patient."

Amy left fifteen minutes later, still shaking her head and muttering. Bunny's smile grew as Amy's car pulled out. Brent knew his meals were covered. Amy had hung up on his repetitive question of who was coming.

Pushing off the counter she leaned against, Bunny put in Brent's order. She had thirty minutes to prepare. Thirty delicious minutes to plan the man's fate. He offered more use of his services. She chuckled thinking which service she'd use first, his tongue, talented fingers and lips, or his eight-inch delight between his legs.

She caught herself in the mirror as she turned to head upstairs. There was a certain glow about her. Well, nothing said a girl—wait, a woman—couldn't enjoy herself sexually as much as a man. Besides, new black lace lingerie awaited its first trial run.

* * * *

The irritating screech grew the longer the receiver remained off the hook. Brent slammed down his beeping phone. How many times did he need to hear "If you'd like to make a call, please hang up and try your call again"? It was clear Amy had hung up on him.

He moved forward, smacking his foot into the entryway's service table. Yelping in pain, he wheeled backwards.

"Damnable chair!" he cursed, scraping another black mark along the narrow hall separating the entryway from the living room.

Clear of the entryway and hall maze, he sat fuming in his living room. His foot hurt like hell. It itched more every time it throbbed, and now it felt like bugs were running up and down the inside of his cast. What he wouldn't give for an unbent coat hanger! He slumped sideways in the wheelchair.

He eyed the offending limb stretched out before him cloaked in white. From mid calf down to half his foot was the culprit—his immobilized ankle. "Two weeks in a wheelchair, and if the bone is mending, then six weeks on crutches with little or no weight on the ankle" rung through his mind. The kicker had been when the x-ray showed he'd sprained his Achilles tendon, too.

"Great," he muttered. His exasperated tone bounced off his bare walls. He'd barely moved in when the call had come. Two weeks of advanced training and continuing education. As a newly placed chief, he still needed instructor certification along with his EMT skills review classes.

"Two more weeks Bunny gets to avoid me." He looked around his living room. A lumpy sofa bed sat along one wall with a table lamp on the floor next to it. His belongings and furniture occupied one corner. Living out of boxes was getting old.

A distant ding caught his attention. At least he could reach the front loading washer and dryer. He didn't want Amy folding or handling his underwear. Her bedside manner and sponge baths sent shivers down his spine. And not in a good way!

He glanced at his watch as he rolled toward the dryer. Forty-five minutes had passed since he'd sent Amy to get his lunch. His stomach rumbled, protesting its emptiness. His luck, Amy had inflated her side of things, and Bunny refused to serve him. Or, maybe she'd sent over to the station for someone to deliver it. He didn't care. His cabinets were bare. He wasn't eating another bowl of Amy's burnt oatmeal or another cold sandwich. Even Tom's cooking would be palatable at this rate.

Opening the dryer door, he slid an empty basket beneath it. He reached inside and grabbed a handful of clothes. Heat seared across his palm and wretched up his fingers. Snapping his head back, he dropped what he held.

Loud persistent raps, interspersed with doorbell rings, sounded from the front door. Thrusting his hand beneath the refrigerator water dispenser, he ran cold water over it and bellowed over his shoulder, "Damn it! Come in! It's unlocked!"

Grabbing the nearest item, he dried his hand. Footsteps approached. He wheeled the chair to face them. He stopped. Bunny stood before him, clad in the skimpiest black lace lingerie he'd seen in a while. *Breathe. Breathe, Brent. Breathe.*

He glanced down at his hands. Oh, fucking shit. What he thought was a towel sure wasn't. How did he explain wiping his hands on his...blue silk briefs? And, the black pair dangling from his blasted toes?

* * * *

Bunny smiled and tried to not burst out laughing. Catching Brent rinsing his hands from the refrigerator water dispenser and drying them on his briefs was funny enough. Add to it his look of dismay and it was like she caught him in the act. Picking up the briefs hanging from his foot, she asked, "Need help changing 'em?"

She watched him work his throat twice, trying to swallow. He opened his mouth to speak. Nothing followed. He tried twice more to answer. A few stammered sounds and fragmented syllables rolled out. She'd never seen him at a loss for words. She wondered if he was all right until she caught the tinge of red flushing his cheeks.

Sitting the bag containing his lunch on the nearby kitchen table, she moved closer. Her own temperature rose several degrees as she caught him giving her the once-over. Maneuvering him away from the small kitchen area, she sat on his lap and closed his mouth. She traced his lips with her finger and winked.

His hot breath mingled with hers as their lips met. Even though he remained still, confidence ballooned within her. His growing hardness nudged her. She squirmed slightly before her tongue darted in and out of his mouth, silently telling him what she hoped for.

* * * *

Brent's hands went to Bunny's hips. Her precarious seat was getting hotter and hornier. What man could resist a woman in black lace? Hell, it was *nice*. His motor raced from the moment she showed up in her attire. Overdrive kicked in when she took the lead and showed him how much she wanted him. The man in him wondered why. His hormones said enjoy.

Rubbing the small of her back, her soft, murmured purrs complemented the rolls and ripples of her muscles beneath his fingers. His palms replaced his fingers, cupping and soothing each tense and stressed muscle he encountered. Her soft gasps and *oh*s told him his touch was welcomed. One more squirm and he'd have one big wet spot to explain.

Scents and taste assaulted his nose and tongue. Such intimacy shared, and yet, she remained aloof. He could no longer ignore the loud clamor of his raging hormones. He pulled his tongue from hers, separating their lips a short distance. His hands fell to her waist, steadying her, ready to prevent flight if necessary.

"I need to know why..." His words hung between them unfinished as her mouth reclaimed his. Was she caught up in the heat of passion? Or avoiding and hiding? He didn't need or want a mercy roll in the hay. What had Amy said?

* * * *

Bunny drew back as Brent's words registered. *Why?* That was the question she kept asking herself over and over. Her eldest, Christy, knew about New York. She was glad for Bunny. Christy's question mirrored hers and Brent's. *Why now and with Brent?* She smiled, remembering her daughter's red face at her uncensored reply during her visit while Brent was gone.

"I like the way you scratch my internal itch?" she offered, wrapping her arms around Brent's neck.

Brent's snort and short chuckle said she had his attention. She knew he partially accepted her off-the-wall response. His eyes keenly watched her.

"Thanks. I like scratching it. You do the same for me."

His hands slid up her sides, fingering the edges of her bra. She felt him grow harder as he cupped her breasts. Twin cutouts exposed her taut nipples. Small beaded pieces hung from each.

She smiled at his harsh intake. "Like the view, huh?" She wiggled her upper torso, shaking her breasts across his palms.

He dropped his hand. She gasped. It rested between her legs. His short snort and wicked leer said he liked what he found, her crotchless panties. "Oh yeah, I like a lot."

His last word rolled across his tongue like a growling purr. His male dominance ignited, ready to claim his mate. *Mate?* What brought that to mind? His next move stopped her pondering.

* * * *

Brent lightly feathered his fingertips up and down her twin nether lips, pausing mid-way each pass to tweak her clit. Every tug and pull pressed her tighter to him. Holding her fast to him, he teased and stroked her. He loved feeling her hum and throb under his tutelage.

Her parted lips and her softly rasped *yes* told him she was close. He dipped his fingers lower. Her wetness oiled his questing fingers. She sucked in air and leaned against him.

He was sure his unshaven cheek chafed her neck and chest each time she arched her shoulders. Brent pulled back. Red splotches and hues lined her skin. Remembering their earlier escapade, he grinned. He continued stroking and tweaking as he nipped her ear and whispered, "I can't resist marking you each time we're together like this."

His grin deepened as goose bumps formed up and down her arms. "Ah, you like my claiming you, eh?"

"Hmmm...yes," Bunny hissed. Her eyes closed, and she squirmed restlessly over him.

Her head lay against him, exposing more of her neck. Her legs tensed as her wetness grew, dampening his pants. Each stroke of her engorged clit pulsed beneath his seeking fingers. She was close to release and her trust in him implicit. As much as he preferred to be buried balls deep in her finding their mutual pleasure, now was not the time.

"I love when you're wet and ready to come. Come for me now," he whispered in her ear. His fingers plucked and stroked her nipple and clit at the same time. He increased pressure with each tweak and rub. Her growing, erratic inhales said she was teetering at the edge.

Moments later, she tensed in his arms amidst her low, throaty vocals. His hands slipped to her waist, supporting her limp-prone position.

* * * *

Bunny inhaled and held her breath. Her heart pounded its echoing beat through her ears and temples. Her mental faculties must not be working. Had she heard him mention love? Still too frazzled and scrambled from her intense orgasm, she let go trying to make sense of things. She'd sort them out later.

"What about you?" she asked, rising unsteadily.

His wry grin greeted her. His eyes lowered. Hers followed. Two large, wet spots dotted his lap in separate areas. Raising her view, Brent's nonchalant shrug plucked her conscience. She'd learned to be a caring, giving lover, not a taker or user. She offered the only response she could think of. "Sorry."

Brent took her hand and squeezed. "No problem, love."

Love? He used the word again. What did he mean by it? There was a look in his eyes, a tenderness or softness she hadn't noticed before. Panic warped over her blissed-out feeling, ramping its acidic affect around her fragile heart. Damn him! How dare he read more into things! All she wanted was to be friends. Wait, how did Christy describe it? Yes, friends with benefits.

Bunny accepted his friendship and his itch-scratching services, which he did very well.

Liar, her inner critic clamored.

She gulped air. Where had that come from? Okay, he was damn good at what he did. She liked and enjoyed his companionship.

No more, she subconsciously scolded. Removing her hand, she smiled. "Your lunch is cold. I'll heat it up." She grabbed the bag and hurriedly circumvented Brent.

* * * *

Brent took in Bunny's agitated movements. Her expression said something was wrong. He'd learned to read her in the months he'd been frequenting Kater's. He wondered if she'd slough it off or if she'd give him an honest answer. He knew she didn't lie. Her overall reputation as a truthful, honoring-her-word businessperson was well known community-wide. Of course, there was a first time for everything. He hoped it wasn't now.

He used her preoccupation with reheating his food to wheel closer to her. He didn't like leaving things unresolved. More than once his therapist pointed this out. Some things he learned to create his own closure for, or let go. This wouldn't be one of them. Catching her hand as she turned, he noticed the tears threatening to spill. His heart clenched. He cared far too much to press her like this. Until he knew for sure what pushed her buttons this time, he wouldn't pursue his current line of thought.

"Are you okay?" he quietly asked, tugging her toward him.

She resisted, before moving nearer. Her chest rose and fell with each agitated breath. She was definitely wound up. Rather than risk her temper or another game of cat and mouse, he decided to let her tell him what she preferred to share.

* * * *

Bunny focused on Brent's hand holding hers. She hated anxiety attacks and the tears they always brought. It'd been years since her last. Brent's use of the word love hit a little too close to home for her. The blasted thing was she didn't know why. She hoped he didn't push for an answer. Right now, one wasn't in the offing.

She raised her eyes to his. Taking a short breath, she answered. "Yes, I'm fine. Frustrated that Amy waited to tell me this for four weeks. She should have told me sooner even though we were sort of staying apart." She pointed to Brent's ankle.

"It happened during our two week hiatus which turned into four thanks to this. I asked everyone to keep quiet, especially Amy." Brent knocked on his cast.

Bunny smiled and looked at the living room filled with half-opened boxes. Her gaze landed on the open sofa sleeper. "Somehow I don't believe you traded your bed for that."

Brent's sheepish grin twinkled his eyes. She grinned in return. "Okay, this one I want to hear."

Brent licked his lips and opened his mouth to speak. The microwave dinged, drawing their attention.

"I'm hungry." His stomach growled noisily as she removed the food.

"Talk to me as you eat." She placed the dishes before him.

Several bites later, he wiped his mouth. Setting his fork down, he turned to face her. "Amy told you what happened?"

Bunny donned one of Brent's shirts in lieu of her trench coat. She perched on a nearby stool. "She told me enough. What's with the chair?"

Brent's sigh filled the kitchen. He gripped the chair's arms as he spoke. "Seems I did it good. Ankle broke cleanly. I sprained my damn Achilles tendon, too."

"And?" She waited for him to continue.

"Between the breaks and the sprain, this ankle won't bear any weight on it, and crutches are out of the picture for the next two to three weeks. I can't get upstairs in this, can I?" He smacked at the chair with his open hand. "Damn it!" Brent shook his hand and scowled. "See what I mean. This friggin' chair bites."

Bunny drew her mouth tight, trying hard to not snicker or grin. Brent's slow burn of frustration came through loud and clear. His sarcastic tone and word emphasis told of his impatience and agitation. Being male, he warred against the constraints. Bunny inhaled deeply. She knew what needed to be done. First, she needed a few more answers.

Clearing her throat, she drew Brent's attention away from his silent sulk. "I've got a couple of questions."

"Oh?" His concerned look tugged at her. Was he trying to be stoic like Derrick had been when he'd gotten hurt on duty?

Patting his hand, she continued. "How serious is this?" She pointed to his cast.

His chest expanded with his breath, and a disgusted sigh followed. She'd hit on a key issue. Settling back on the stool, she folded her arms and waited.

"It's broke in two places and swollen. Until the swelling's down, the doctor isn't sure if I'll need surgery or not. I might not be able to keep my job if I lose mobility or flexibility with it," he said in a stiff voice.

Bunny heard the worry in his voice. "When is your next appointment?'

"I had one earlier this week. Things appear to be healing, but he wants to wait another two to three weeks and x-ray again."

"Uh-huh." Bunny picked up Brent's dishes and placed them in the dishwasher. "I see only one option."

Chapter Nine

"You're moving back in with me." Bunny closed the dishwasher, setting it to run. She glanced at the kitchen wall clock. Dinner rush didn't start for a few more hours. She had time to convince...who? Brent? Herself? Both of them?

"I'm what?" Brent's voice boomed over the counter separating them. Bunny realized he was grumpy as well as worried.

Her last thought made her smile. If she wasn't sure, why suggest it? *That little four letter word—love. It gives you the willies.* Refusing to listen to her nagging subconscious further, she rounded the counter and stopped before a glaring Brent. Hands on her hips, she glowered back, resisting the urge to shake her finger at him and yell. She inhaled and counted. Somewhere between seven and ten, she exhaled.

She took one stride toward him. He wheeled backward. Two more, and he was between the counter and the boxes. "Brent, it's either me or Amy. Take your pick." She smiled at his grimace when she mentioned Amy. "So what's your choice?"

"How you and she are best friends is beyond me. I can't take another attack of Attila the Hun's cooking or sponge baths. Does that answer your question?"

His acerbic tone gave her new insight and appreciation for Brent. He survived Amy's temper tantrums and her lousy bedside manner. His sullen look reminded her of his bad malaise. Sighing, she moved back.

"Brent, I know you hate being incapacitated." She picked up an empty box and sat it on his lap. "At my place, you can work at the station on files and paperwork. Amy can assist without either of you killing or screaming at the other."

A twinkle flashed through his eyes. "Yes, Amy can be caustic at times. None of us are angelic saints."

"You said a mouthful on that one. She's one of my best first-aid technicians."

Brent's smile made her smirk. She hoped the prospect of being near the station and limited work access eased his downer mood.

"I've got a question," he said, wheeling behind her as she sorted through boxes.

"Yes, what?" She avoided looking at him, hoping he wouldn't start dissecting her motives.

"Getting up and down the stairs at your place isn't going to be any easier than here. Am I camping out in the kitchen?"

His short chuckle made her laugh and snort.

"No, unless you want to fight Ben off. I hear he's dangerous wielding his meat cleaver." She dropped several articles of clothing and toiletries in the box occupying his lap. His hand clasped hers.

"Seriously, where am I laying my head till my wheels are no more?" His curious gaze gave her pause.

She reached for the box. His hand covered hers. "I refuse to compromise yours or Kate's reputations."

She gulped as her heart skipped a beat or two. No one had shown such genuine concern for her since Derrick. Guilt inched further up her back. The man was racking up one hell of a set of redeeming qualities.

Licking her lips, she answered. "Phillip's room is large enough to accommodate your needs and give you room to roll around. The shower has a bench in it, and if I remember where I put it, I've a waterproof cast cover to use while bathing."

"Are you sure about putting me up in *your* home? What about gossip?"

Bunny glanced over her shoulder and leaned closer. "I'm of age. How about you?"

Brent's weak chuckle said he wasn't buying it.

"Look, what I do after hours behind my closed doors is my business."

"I agree. People love to talk, and Jameston is a close-knit community." Brent's shrug pushed her ire higher.

"Most of Jameston could care less. A few will speculate. I'm not worried about them. Okay?" Her exasperated tone startled even her.

* * * *

Brent smiled. The girl had spunk. He released her hand. "I understand."

Bunny grabbed the box off his lap. "How much of your stuff do want to take with you?"

"I have clean clothes in the dryer and another load in the washer. A few books and some CDs should do. What about internet?"

"Whole place is wired. Where's your laptop?"

"At the station. Amy can bring it over later."

Grabbing a basket, Brent opened the washer and pulled out the damp load. "Do you mind emptying the dryer?"

He snuck a quick glance. She opened the dryer and took out several pieces. Her eyes met his.

"Don't get any ideas, buddy," she teased. "Just because I'm handling your unmentionables doesn't grant you privileges. Got it?"

Her wink and grin told him what he needed to know. She made her decision and was fine with it. Clarity filled him. Bunny knew where she stood and recognized her limits. A new respect flowed through him along with a new understanding.

* * * *

Brent cussed under his breath. Six weeks sitting and doing nothing was beginning to wear on him. How much more could he take? Ben refused to let him help, and Bunny kept telling him to relax and enjoy his time off. Even when Kate was off visiting her sister, Bunny had been more of a nursemaid than a playmate. Now Kate was back. And he was sleeping alone again.

"Hi, Mr. Stephens." Kate called out as she passed him sitting in the doorway to Bunny's office. "I'm sorry to hear about your leg."

Brent nodded. How much did Kate know? Had she drilled Bunny, asking all kinds of questions? How long before Kate asked him point blank what he was doing here? Maybe he was old fashioned by current social standards. He didn't feel comfortable sharing the intimate details of his and Bunny's relationship with Kate.

Brent opened his mouth. Bunny's call caught both their attentions. "Kate, are you home?"

"Yes, Mom." Bunny's approaching footsteps echoed down the hall.

Kate edged past Brent and moved toward the open door at the end of the hall. The entry led to Bunny's private domain.

"Brent, your doctor called. He's referred you to an orthopedic specialist in two weeks."

"Thanks," he mumbled and wheeled into the café's dining area. "I'm going to my office and check on things. Call me when dinner's ready."

* * * *

Bunny hesitated, unsure how to reply. Something was eating at Brent. His hot, hard "damn" and "ouch" propelled her forward. "Kate, I'll be back in a moment."

She reached the door as it swung closed behind Brent. His slumped shoulders and tousled hair spoke volumes. The man was worried. Cranky and full of ire, he worked his way down the short sidewalk separating the two buildings. Dare she go after him?

She started out the door with his name on the tip of her tongue. Too late. Tony and Tom reached him first. Their mouths moved rapidly, indicating a conversation. Bunny shrugged and went back in. There'd be time for talk later, she hoped.

"Mom," Kate called out, "can I ask you something?"

Bunny followed the voice and found Kate at their kitchen table. A puzzled look filled her eyes. Pulling out a chair, she sat. "What is it?"

"What's up with Mr. Stephens?"

"I'm not sure what you're asking about."

Kate's eye roll made her smile. She'd learned the hard way to ask Kate questions before she spoke or to get a clearer explanation. Today's kids knew more than they let on.

"It's like he's mad or doesn't like being here. I don't get it."

Bunny inhaled sharply. How much had Christy said during Kate's visit? She waited, making sure Kate was done.

"Honey, remember how active Brent is. To have that stop has probably upset him. What did you and Christy talk about?"

Kate flipped open her geometry book and a notebook. Bunny counted to twenty, admonishing herself for opening a door that could lead into a potentially dangerous discussion. "Christy quizzed me on Mr.—Brent—him. She wanted to know if I liked him and what I knew."

"And?" Memories flashed through Bunny's mind. Similar scenes as Kate grew up. One stuck out above all others, the time Christy told Kate the facts of life. Bunny sighed. She loved Christy a lot, but sometimes the girl's mouth could ratchet into overdrive.

Kate smiled. "You can breathe, Mom. She said little about Brent, except he was here and his leg was hurt. I surprised her when I said I knew you'd gone to New York with him."

Bunny nodded. Even grown, her girls still tried to out-do the other.

"Let's set the record straight. Brent is staying in Phillip's old room. His place is on two levels. Here, he'll be close to work, and I can help him as needed."

"Mom." Kate gave an all-knowing grin. "It's okay if there's more to it. I'm eighteen. I like Brent."

Bunny stared, startled by Kate's blatant remark. How much did Kate know? "I'm glad you like Brent. What do you mean if there's more?"

"Come on, Mom. I saw him kiss you. You've acted different since you came back from New York. I'm glad you have a boyfriend. Stop worrying. Even Phillip agrees."

Bunny froze as she rose from her chair. *Christy and her big mouth!* What had she told her brother? Slowly sitting back down, she faced Kate. "Okay, Miss Full-of-Surprises. Spill it. Everything. Christy's been at it again."

Kate laughed and patted her arm. "Phillip visited while I was at Christy's. He quizzed us about you. Christy's always been very close to you. So Phillip kept at her 'til she told him about Brent."

"Crap," slipped from Bunny's lips as her hand flew to her mouth.

"No, Mom," Kate answered. "Christy said you had a boyfriend named Brent, and she was happy for you. I added he worked next door to us and took you to New York for your birthday."

Bunny unclenched her hands. "Phillip didn't push for more information?" Her son could be overprotective.

"Nope. Christy told him if he wanted to know more, call you or come visit."

Bunny's shoulders relaxed. She felt the stress ebb its way down her back, loosening the kinks and tense muscles along the way. At least Brent wasn't facing the Kater Inquisition yet or a virtual public tar and feathering by her children. "Kate, I'll be back soon. I'm going to check on Brent. Check with Ben, and see if he needs any help."

Kate's reply bounced off her preoccupied mind. Brent's dour mood concerned her.

* * * *

Brent accepted Tony's assistance into his office. It felt good to be back at work, even in a limited way. Tom's status report brought him up to speed on shifts and current issues. Amy even spoke to him civilly. Things were looking up. *Were they?* His conscience pricked him.

He knew a tough choice was coming. One he'd not given much thought to, ever. Christ, how did one make a life-changing decision when every piece of the future seemed uncertain? Even during therapy, he'd never wavered from his determination to return to his chosen profession. Why was now different?

Out of the corner of his eye, he saw why. Stark white in color, sticking out in front of him, taunting and unyielding in its presence, was why. His damn ankle. Another MRI would tell if he had severe soft-tissue damage. Another reason for possible surgery. God, he hated this immobility. Sore arms from crutching would be a welcome relief to this chair.

Two quick raps brought him back from his thoughts. Combing both hands through his hair, he turned. It was probably Tony with coffee and a snack. He bade the knocker enter.

Bunny's worried face peered around the door. What did she want? Brent tried to smile. His heart wasn't in it.

"Hey." Bunny greeted him and closed the door behind her. Stepping around him, she leaned on his desk, facing him. "You left suddenly. What's up?"

Brent sighed. He hadn't slept well since Kate returned home. He missed Bunny snuggling against him until they fell asleep holding each other. Peanuts had taken to sleeping with him, but yowled and fussed each time he turned over. His world was upside down. How did he communicate this without sounding like he was whining?

"Talk to me, please?" The question floated between them. Did she really want to hear what he had to say?

A loud knock broke their mutual stare. "Come in,' Brent called out.

"Two coffees and cookies, Chief. I saw Ms. Bunny come in." Tony sat the tray on the desk.

"Thanks, Tony."

"You bet. Yell if you need more." Tony latched the door behind him.

Stirring his coffee, Brent gathered his thoughts. A small voice pinged his conscience. Maybe time for an open discussion had come. "Pull up a chair. This is gonna take a few."

He waited until Bunny settled back in her chair. Her fidgeting told of her impatience.

"Please hear me out," Brent began, taking Bunny's hand. "I've got a lot going on in my head. Dr. Sanders is not sure if everything is healing as it should."

Bunny's grip tightened. She gasped.

"That's why he called in the specialist. Once the swelling's down more, I need another MRI to verify soft tissue damage."

"That's not good," Bunny mumbled.

"No, it's not. Damn thing is, unless the tissue and sprain are mending, the bones could separate and re-break with no support. Thus surgery and more cutting."

Bunny slid to the edge of her chair. "What else?"

"If..." He swallowed hard. His throat went dry every time he put the two words together. "If Sanders is correct..." He licked his lips. "Permanent damage. Limited disability."

Bunny's arms enfolded him. *God, he loved her.* Inwardly he yelled yahoo, and his heart palpitated. Dare he verbalize his feelings? How would she react if he told her? He couldn't stop his feelings even if she wanted him to. Wrapping his arms around her, he mouthed the words, waiting to see her reaction.

Bunny pulled away. "Did you say something?" Her stare cut into him.

She knew he'd said something. Had she heard him? Better acknowledge the deed and not the words. He wanted some space before he told her. "Yeah, a quick prayer." Bunny smiled and caressed his cheek.

Brent pushed back from his desk, picking up his coffee. "How'd Kate take my being there?"

Bunny sat on his desk, holding her cup, swinging her crossed legs. She stared past him as if her thoughts took her back in time. "She surprises me still. One moment my baby. The next all grown up."

"They do grow up fast," he said.

Her gaze returned to him. "Kate knew you were here before she got home. Christy's loose lips strike again. Well, semi-loose. Phillip even knows." Shaking her head, she sipped her coffee.

"When does the tar and feathering committee arrive?"

"Won't, can't and knows better." Bunny's muffled laugh indicated there was more.

He munched a cookie and waited.

"Kate reported for the three of them. They're fine with Mom having a boyfriend. Though I'm fond of Christy's description— friends with benefits."

Brent swallowed hard. The cookie stuck in his throat, fighting his plummeting heart for space. His heart fell to the bottom of his stomach and washed up on its acidy shore. Grabbing his coffee, he gulped. Thank God it had cooled.

"Are you okay?" Bunny asked, jumping up.

"Yes. Dry throat and cookie war. I'm fine now."

She sat, watching him. He had to get things under control or he'd be blurting out what she apparently didn't want to hear.

Picking up a pile of papers close to her, he redirected her focus again. "I've got reports to read and sign off on for Tom. It'll take me a couple of hours to get through this." He thumbed the stack. "How long 'til dinner?"

Bunny glanced at her watch. "You can eat with Kate and me, or I can send Ben over with something. Your call."

"Send Ben over" rested on his lips. But why should he have to give up eating with Bunny? The more time they spent together, the stronger he cemented their bond and showed her how compatible they were. Having Kate solidly and favorably in his corner wouldn't hurt, either. He liked Kate. The staff referred to her as their adopted little sister.

"I'll eat with you and Kate. Send her over or call me when it's time."

Bunny stood and kissed Brent's cheek. "All right. Don't eat too many cookies and spoil your dinner," she added, taking one with her.

The click of the door closing behind her drew Brent from his thoughts. He halfway expected to see her still standing there. He cracked the door, wanting to make sure she truly departed. He needed to talk and think out loud. There was one person he trusted to be objective. Brent picked up the phone and dialed.

Three rings later, a deep familiar voice answered. "Cupertino's."

"Hey, bro." Brent's voice cracked. Clearing his throat, he continued. "Damn cookie."

Randy's warm laugh rumbled through the phone. "Somehow I didn't think you'd hit puberty again, Squeaky."

Brent's laugh joined Randy's. His teenage nickname brought back a rush of memories. "Been a few years since then, for sure. How are Terra and the kids?"

Conversation flowed as Randy brought Brent up to speed on the family. "You're not one to call to shoot the shit," Randy challenged. "An email is your norm. What's up?"

Brent heard his sigh echo over the phone. Leave it to Randy to cut to the chase. "I've got a couple of questions."

"Oh? Okay." Randy's quizzical tone said he had some, too.

"Remember when Dad pulled out his high school ring and reminisced about asking Mom to go steady?"

"Boy, do I. He talked about finding the right girl and settling down. Told us to go slow and listen to our hearts, not our groins."

"I remember how proud he and Mom were when you asked for Mom's old engagement ring after you asked Terra to marry you. I wish I'd done them as proud with Marta, but I failed." Brent knuckled his eyes. A tear slipped past.

Randy's long sigh filled the quiet space left by Brent's last statement.

"Brent, you couldn't help what happened with you and Marta. Dad told me he hoped you could reconcile. He never held it against you. I'm sorry he died before he could tell you."

"I know. Mom told me repeatedly. I think it's finally sunk in. 'Cuz..." Brent's voice trailed off.

Chapter Ten

"You found her?" Randy asked.

"What makes you think that?" Brent countered. Had he become that readable to even his brother?

"Brent," Randy stated, his voice quieter in tone, "if you have, I'm happy for you. Something's got you unnerved. I can't help unless you tell me."

Brent silently counted forward and backwards. Unsure of where to start, he chose the first words entering his mind. "You know I bought a place."

"Yeah, you needed to work on it."

"Well, it compounded and delays arose. I ended up in temporary housing. I moved in six weeks ago."

"Further complications?" Randy questioned, finishing Brent's thought as the phone grew quiet.

"You might say that. Remember the summer you broke your foot playing ball?"

"Oh man, Squeaky! Did you fall painting? How bad is it?"

Brent snorted and heavily exhaled. "Broke my ankle." He explained what he faced. "It boils down to disability or longer recuperation. Either way, I'm on limited duty and facing potential major changes."

"What kind of change?"

"Give up firefighting." Brent's gut wrenched, knotting tighter as he said "give up".

"Do you know this for sure?" Randy's response worried Brent. He'd called Randy because he needed someone levelheaded to talk to.

"No, not yet. My doctor discussed the possibility. He suggested I prepare myself for it, given the complexity of the injury."

Randy's exasperated sigh burned Brent's ear. "And you're ready to quit? Roll over and give up? What the *hell* has happened to you, Squeaky?"

Brent drummed his fingers hard against his desk. A few taunts and references to his coltish teens were fine. Randy was pushing it, and he wasn't taking any more.

"Enough with the *Squeaky* stuff, okay?"

"I'll quit when my brother stops whining like a child."

"Damn it, Randy!" Brent growled.

"Yes, that's the man I know. The fighter and conqueror. Crap, Brent, 9-11 didn't stop you. Don't let this." His breathing told Brent he listened, waiting for an answer.

"I wish it were that easy, bro. There's something else." Brent paused, wanting Randy to ask him about it.

"Spill your guts. I'm listening." Randy's clipped, even tone emphasized his concern.

"I'm in love. And she probably doesn't love me back." Brent filled Randy in on Bunny. "We got back from New York, and it hit me. Thoughts of us making my place a home. I'm back at her place until I'm on crutches. She hugged me today, and the word 'love' almost spilled out."

"Now I get why you brought up the family. You're thinking about settling down with this one."

Several minutes more of brotherly banter followed. A rap on Brent's door interrupted.

"Brent, it's Kate." Her smiling face peeked around the door. "Mom says come and get it. I'm supposed to help you back."

"Give me a couple of minutes. Go see Tony. He mentioned having something for you."

"Brent, she has kids?" Randy's voice brought him back to current.

"Yes, three. Kate is the youngest. Why?"

"Are you ready to be a stepdad? What about having your own?"

Leave it to Randy to ask the hard-core questions. He didn't mince words. He had a good head on his shoulders and played fairly. These were two of the key reasons Brent trusted him implicitly.

"Bunny has a say if there are more. It doesn't matter to me either way. As to being a stepdad, that's up to her kids." Brent waited for Randy's reaction. Hearing none, Brent continued.

"Randy, I've gotta run. What one solid piece of advice can you give me?" Brent gripped the phone.

"Know I love ya no matter what. You're my brother. Follow your heart and gut. If both agree, they won't lead you wrong. She must be one special lady."

"She is. Thanks, Randy. We'll talk soon. Love ya, too." Brent hung up the phone and turned. He found Kate watching him.

"I didn't mean to intrude." Kate's voice warbled.

"No problem. Are you upset by what you heard?"

"Yes and no. To hear my mom talked about is freaky. What you said isn't. I think she's special, too." Kate smiled, returning Brent's smile.

Taking Kate's hand, Brent squeezed it. "Let's keep this our secret. Your mom might not like being talked about."

Kate winked and laughed. "How do you think Kater's got so well known? Word of mouth, according to Mom. I'm sure she's used to it."

"Just the same, let me tell her about it. I did the gabbing so best I claim the deed. Okay?"

Kate opened the door wider. "Mom said something about pot roast, mashed potatoes, and honey yeast rolls. And my favorite dessert, Ben's real rum pumpkin spice cake. "

Brent's stomach growled with each word. "I think the vote is in. Let's go eat."

* * * *

Bunny pushed back from her desk. Folding the bank statement, she relaxed, sliding down into the padded office chair's cushions. Flush financially and with holiday business to see them through the ensuing winter, she knew money wasn't her worry.

Both Brent and Kate were getting along well. His tutoring her in geometry helped tremendously. Kate's GPA had come up two points. Even now, the two of them were arguing—oops—practicing Kate's debate speech. So Bunny wondered what had her so melancholy?

Love, her psyche crowed.

"Yeah, right," she muttered. "Why should that bother me?"

'Cuz he said it.

"'Cuz he said it," she repeated aloud.

The thought puzzled her. When had he? She didn't remember...Crap, he had!

She thought he used his terms of endearment as part of his casual speech. He called Kate hon from time to time as most southerners did. She figured he'd picked up the local vernacular.

His hurried whispers as he hugged her each night made sense now. Was this his way of blessing her? How attached had he become?

The more she thought about it, the more her heart raced. Getting attached to someone, she wasn't sure she liked that. She loved Christy, Phillip, and Kate. Knew they felt the same way. Hell, she even loved Amy. Somehow she doubted Brent meant it that way.

"Take a deep breath," she told herself. "You could ask him what he means by it or if he said it."

You're too scared, also, her inner critic chastised. *What would you do if he said he meant it? Run? Back away? Coward!*

Covering her face with her hands, she leaned forward, putting her elbows on her desk. Kate's called out "Night, Mom" followed by Brent's "Sweet dreams, Kate" pulled Bunny from her musings. A hard knock on her office door startled her.

"Bunny?" Brent's muffled voice sounded outside the door. Grabbing a compact mirror from the middle desk drawer, she checked her reflection. She was a bit flushed in the cheeks. Otherwise, she looked fine. Running a hand through her hair, she stuffed the mirror back in the drawer.

"Hang on. I'm coming," she called out, drawing two quick, deep breaths. She counted to five and opened the door.

"Hey, what's up?" she asked, her look going straight to Brent's face. His warm smile washed over her. He wheeled forward.

Holding up her hands, she tittered. "Haven't we done this before?"

"Oh, I believe that turnabout is fair play. So my turn now." He continued toward her. His grin turned into a lecherous leer as she stepped back.

"Brent, what is with you?"

Leaning forward, he grabbed her wrist and tugged. Caught between the corner of her desk and the nearby file cabinet, she didn't have much room. "Look you per—"

"Oh yes, I'll make you purr," Brent teased, tumbling her across his lap.

"Brent, Kate will hear us." Bunny pushed against him, trying to rise.

"No she won't, unless you refuse to kiss me. No kiss, you get swatted. What'll it be, woman?" He puckered his lips and winked at her.

The glint in his eyes spoke of the fire simmering below his waist. The heat was catchy. She fanned herself. He made her hot. Hot with need and desire. She enjoyed the vigorous partner Brent was.

But with Kate's bedroom close by and Ben hadn't left yet, she wasn't taking any chances. She rose part way and turned. Brent's hand closed around her wrist and tugged. Falling forward, she reached for his other hand. He caught her, easing her on her stomach across his lap.

A solid swat sound filled the office. Her ass grew warm as three more followed.

"I asked you, woman, what'll be?" Brent swatted her ass again, adding more warmth to the warmth already pooling in her nether region, and making her nipples swell.

"Taking charge, are you?" she asked, her voice taking on its own assertive tone. She moved against him, attempting to leave his tenuous hold.

* * * *

Brent moved his hand lower, tracing the slight v her parted legs created. Her breasts rubbed his upper thigh, coming closer to his crotch each time she squirmed. Glad he'd forgone briefs under his jogging pants, his cock nudged its questing head on her.

"Hold still, woman, and accept your consequences." Leaning his weight on her, he held her in place. He stroked firmer and deeper between her legs. Her heat grew with each pass. A muffled groan reached him as his hand cupped her.

"Brent," she panted, her engorged nipples chafing his covered cock.

"Like it a bit rough, eh?" He forced his hand between her legs, fully cupping her, rocking his hand tighter against her. His other hand slid over her shoulder, and finding her taut nipple, he captured it with his thumb and forefinger. Alternating each motion, he spoke of his intent. Each elicited moan and vocalization raised his desire. He repeated his question and ceased his actions. "I asked do you like it a bit rough."

Her chest heaved against his legs as she drew a ragged breath. Raising her head, her desire-laden eyes grabbed him. She licked her lips and answered. "Yes, I like what you do to me."

He grew harder at her gasped reply. Pre-cum leaked out and over his cock head.

"Now, woman, where's my kiss?" He growled, swiftly sitting her upright.

Bunny fell against his body, wrapping her arms around him. Thrusting his hand in her hair, he tangled strands around his fingers and firmly tugged, forcing her head back. Holding her chin with his other hand, he brushed her lips with his. A soft groan escaped her parted lips.

Capturing her bottom lip between his teeth, he worried its edge. Each nibble he soothed with a brief kiss until she opened and pressed her mouth to his, bidding him enter. Slipping his tongue over her welcoming portal, he released her chin. He dragged his fingers in feather-light touches along her jaw line. Every tremble and sound she made reached deeper into his heart, burgeoning desire.

She's the one, his inner voice confirmed. *Love's come knockin' at your door. Open up and let it in.* A thread of Randy's conversation echoed along. "You're thinking about settling down with this one."

Settling down...What did it mean? Living together? Separate places? Exclusive dating?

Boy, what are you worrying about? You've got a hot, horny woman in your arms. Worry about details later!

Brent broke the kiss and drew in a deep breath. "Unless we slow down some, we're gonna do it here." Holding Bunny tight, he seated her facing forward, one leg straddling his out stretched leg. Her other dangled between his. With short, swift turns, he wheeled them out of the office. "Great, I can't see worth shit. How do I drive this thing?" Bunny's snorted snicker made him stop. "Okay smart mouth, what's your suggestion?"

"I suspect if I stood up, we'd have more to explain than you teaching me how to steer." Her muffled laugh widened his grin.

"I must say you're a quick study and an apt student. Any further insights?" he asked, nipping the base of her neck closest to her shoulder.

"I'll be your eyes, and you steer," she offered. He swore there was a lilting tease in her voice.

"All right, woman, I put our fate and my foot in your capable sight." He maneuvered forward.

Ten minutes later, no worse for wear, they wheeled into Phillip's bedroom. Ben's offer of a horn and a guide dog renewed their mutual mirth. Ben's laughing good night as he departed left them blushing and giggling like teenagers

"Our final destination, madam, waits before us." Brent hoped he pointed in the right direction. Bunny's soft "goodness" told him she'd seen it. He owed Tony and Ben.

* * * *

Bunny stood, her knees trembling. She blinked, waiting for the scene before her to evaporate. So perfect and yet surreal. Brent wheeled next to her. He loosely held her hand.

Red satin sheets with rose pink blankets graced the bed. Two dozen roses in various vases lined the perimeter of the bed. Flameless tea lights flickered near the window and nightstand. An open box of Godiva chocolates sat in middle of the bed. Bunny swallowed, once...twice...and a third time as she turned.

Two small sponge brushes sat near a small fondue pot heated by a Sterno can. An open jar of chocolate body paint sat nearby. Dropping Brent's hand, she stepped closer. Another jar sat near the open one. She picked it up and read White Chocolate. The other read Dark Chocolate.

Arms slid around her hips and squeezed. "I hope you like." Brent's voice vibrated across her lower back.

She stepped from his embrace. Turning to face him, she went slack-jawed. The man was practically naked. He'd worked his jogging pants down past his crotch. The bright red male bikini briefs hanging from his casted foot caught her attention. He wiggled his toes as best he could at her. Movement drew her gaze higher.

Brent moved his hands from his crotch. His cock wore a top hat and black tie with an envelope propped against it. Bunny moved toward him, smiling at his cleverness. The man made sex fun and interesting. She reached for the envelope. His cock moved. Glancing upward, she caught his lecherous grin and wink. She bit her cheek to keep from snickering. Opening the envelope, she emptied its contents—four condoms with a small folded piece of paper. The printing read: "Think we can use 'em all up in one night? I'm up for the challenge. Are you?"

"Are you double-dog daring me?" she asked. She removed the miniature hat and tie from his cock. She softly squeezed and worked her hand downwards.

Brent's tight-lipped groan and jerky hip movement warmed her.

"So you are daring me. Let's see how well you hold up." She released him and walked toward the door.

Squeaks from Brent's chair told her he moved, watching her. She paused at the door. Taking her time, she counted to thirty, slowly closing it. She knew she blocked his view. He had no idea what she was doing.

"Bunny?" His voice cracked.

Quietly, she turned the lock. Her mind calculated how many ways her internal itch needed scratching. She faced him and closed the space separating them. Placing her fingers over his mouth, she leaned forward and whispered in his ear her sensual intent.

"You're mine for the next few hours. Mine to do with as I please. My toy. Are you game?" Running her fingers up and down his neck, she worried his earlobe with her lips. She felt his gulp and rising heat each time her tongue soothed her nip. Pulling back, she moved around him. She captured his chin and held his gaze firm. "No words. Just a bob or shake. Do you agree?"

Stepping away from him, she unfastened three buttons on her blouse and leaned down. She watched Brent's eyes widen. Her sly wink and wicked grin response got another answer. His low, naughty laugh followed.

Her demi bra and the view of her cleavage got results. Standing up, she walked to the nightstand. She took her time unbuttoning her blouse. What did one do with a gift of surrendered control? He knew bits and pieces of her favorite fantasies and she his. The scene before her confirmed he wasn't scared of using the information.

Dipping her finger in the chocolate, a delightful image flashed through her mind. The liquid sweetness's temperature registered tolerable and warm. She opened the jar marked white chocolate. Its texture, a bit thicker than the pot's contents, made her grin. Oh, yes this was going to be fun. Humming a lewd ditty from her youth, she opened the nightstand drawer.

Bright colors greeted her. She rummaged through the contents. Glancing over her shoulder, she confirmed he hadn't moved. Her turn to leer. A quick peek at the items her hand held widened her grin. She pulled the items to her and shut the drawer.

Sassily walking toward him, she dangled her prizes in front of her. With her free hand, she unclasped the single closure of her bra. Brent's eyes moved from her full hand to her busy one. His throat moved as he swallowed. The closer she got, the more evident it became she was getting to him.

His normal attentive gaze focused more, taking in her movement. The topper was his cock. Pre-cum glistened on and over its turgid tip. She couldn't resist such a gift. Shoving her bra cups aside, she fondled and tweaked her breasts. His cock jerked and more cum oozed over its edge.

"Well, well, your non-verbal communication needs no enhancement, does it?" Her free hand encircled him mid-shaft and pumped upwards. Draping her silken scarves around his neck, she pursued her lips, drew his gift deep into her mouth, and flicked her tongue rapidly.

* * * *

Brent's hands fisted in her hair and held her in place. He pumped his heated arousal deep in her mouth and pulled back. She permitted his infraction to go on several moments longer. Catching his hand with hers, Bunny clasped his wrist. Quickly up righting herself, she dragged her silk scarf down his chest.

"Tsk tsk, bad boy," she chided, taunting his cock with the scarf's fringe. "Give me your hand."

Brent hesitated.

"You surrendered, remember?" She looped one end around the wrist she held. "Give it over," she commanded, pointing at her desired object. Brent shrugged and laid his free wrist on his bound one.

Bunny firmly knotted both ends of the scarf together. "Don't pull too much or you'll hard knot them."

Brent nodded his understanding.

"If I help, can you get into the bed?" she asked, moving him closer to the bed. Brent's short nod said he could. Raising his hands to her shoulder, Bunny steadied him. Two hops and a precarious totter found him where she wanted him, laying on his back spread eagle. Tugging his sweats lower, she eased them over his cast and off his other leg. She tossed them up to the head of the bed. "Just in case we might need them, but I doubt we will.

Knotting four more scarves, two each, she tied each ankle and loosely fastened the free ends to the bed frame. Stroking her hand over his balls and cock, she announced his fate.

"I'm hungry." She wet her fingertips with his sticky dew and traced her lips, licking them. "Hmmm. Salty goodness. Yes, a hunger for..." She paused, catching his gaze.

She turned her back to him. Inhaling twice, she worked to bring her volcanic needs under control. Her hands rose to her tight nipples. Twisting and plucking them, she groaned. Her nether lips swelled and parted, leaking her wetness through them.

His slight movements caught her attention. "Thinking of escaping?" she purred, slipping her bra straps and blouse off her shoulders and down her arms. She tossed them aside.

She cupped and palmed her swollen breasts, running her thumbs over and around her erect nipples. Brent's chest rose and fell in rapid breaths, telling her she had his focus. "Tsk tsk, bad boy. Keep misbehaving and I might make you wait longer for your surprise."

Unfastening her waistband, she lowered it to her hips. What would his reaction be when he saw what she wore under her jeans?

She checked the fondue pot's contents. The temperature remained warm and liquidized. Drizzling a generous amount along each nipple and breast top, she stepped close to Brent's head and leaned down. "Gonna be a good boy and help clean this up?"

* * * *

Brent licked his lips and gulped. Where had this lusty dominatrix come from? Was this his Bunny? He wanted to shout out, "Lord, woman, stop teasing me, and let's do it." Instead, he bit his tongue and nodded, wondering where her erotic imagination would take them next.

Her sideways movement drew his gaze. Eye level, two chocolate covered nipples and areolas tempted him. He didn't think his cock could get any harder, but he swore it did. Could he stand much more without his balls beginning to ache? He got his answer.

Rolling his eyes back toward her, he saw it coming. He puckered his lips in anticipation. His tongue tip wedged between them, waited. Was the wait over?

Yes! Sweet chocolate delight assaulted his taste buds followed by firm, womanly flesh rolling along his tongue. Murmured groans and uhmms told of her pleasure. His vixen luxuriated in her power. Good for her.

Her hand found his cock, stroked, once, twice, and dropped to his balls. Cupping them, her whispers reached him. "Poor baby needs attention."

Brent eagerly nodded. It wasn't polite to talk with one's mouth full. He was too busy licking and suckling every inch of Bunny's chocolate-drizzled flesh.

Drawing back, she toweled her chest with his briefs. Her wink and grin said her erotic lust took them in a new direction. She wiped his face and granted him permission to speak.

"How much more do you think I can withstand?"

"As much as I care to dish out?" Her saucy tone spiked her question. The heated spark lighting her eyes indicated he'd soon find out.

She stepped back and commanded him to watch. Twice, she traced the zipper holding her slowly sinking jeans closed. On the next upward flow, she tugged the tab downward. Strips of red and black lace greeted his gaze. Oh temptress unleashed! Was she wearing what he thought she was? Her eyes caught his. Their deep blue hue sparkled each time he licked his lips or groaned. He'd set free a lusting, wanton female. And...

Her hands shoved her jeans down. Brent gasped. The minx shimmied in delight as she bent to remove her pants.

Black lace thong panties accented with red lace-covered elastic adorned her pelvis. His hands itched to fondle and swat the two pert cheeks she wiggled before him. All he could do was kiss and nibble. Her muffled giggles told him of her delight.

Bunny swiftly turned. Licking her palm, she grasped Brent's cock tip and stroked downward. "I think it's time for tar and feathering."

Brent jerked upward. His restraints held firm.

Chapter Eleven

"Wha-a-mrph." Bunny put her hand on Brent's mouth to muffle his yelp. She grinned.

"Calm down." Bunny sat on the edge of the bed where he could easily see her. She held his hand. "You've seen me put chocolate on me. Why not you?"

Brent's ragged breaths slowed. His intent look deepened her grin. "Explain," he said.

His one-word response tickled her. His piqued tone and edgy pitch told of his restrained curiosity and cautious inquisitiveness. She decided to up the stakes.

"I believe in showing rather than telling." Her retort got her desired results as she reached for the fondue pot.

"Showing?" he asked, his voice a bit louder.

"Shh," she admonished. "Wait and see." She winked at him as she watched him over her shoulder.

Dipping both sponge brushes into the appropriate containers, she waited as the excess fluids ran off. Images of her finished tasty concoction flashed through her mind. Smacking her lips and imitating a slurp, she crossed to the bed.

"A little tar." She touched the tip of the sponge to his stomach. She waited for his response. A wicked grin lurched across his lips.

"Gonna have your way with me, woman?" His inhaled hiss followed the sponge's first stroke near the base of his cock. Her short laugh shivered up his shaft and down to his balls. He regained his former hardness and more.

"Oh, yes, perfect," she huskily murmured.

* * * *

Brent lifted his head and gazed at himself. Dark, warm chocolate coated his cock from its glistening pre-cum-coated tip to near his pubic hair.

"Now the feathers," she breathlessly taunted. Dabbles of white chocolate speckled its darker counterpart.

"Perfection." Her purred tone stated her satisfaction. She stood several inches from him, licking liquid remnants from her tools and fingers.

"Hmmm," rolled past her parted lips.

Brent gulped as her warm hand grasped him. "Time to enjoy my handiwork."

She blew hot air over his turgid hardness. How much longer did she plan on fondling him? His balls throbbed with anticipation. Memories of her prior forays crashed through him. Her heated mouth tightened around him, sucking and tasting, working him to a fevered frenzy.

"Woman, have—"

His back arched, and his eyes slammed shut. From tip to where her hand held him, her tongue laved.

"Oh, you like, eh?" She released him and stood.

Panting, he glared at her. Between his aching balls and throbbing cock, his need and patience were reaching fevered proportions. Rustling caught his attention.

She stood before him in unclothed splendor, one lush, naked female. Her grin spoke of more to come.

She wiped her fingers across her mouth, taking with them any fleeting traces of her quick taste. She licked them clean and strolled toward him, wearing a wider grin.

"Woman, have mercy," he groaned. Her hand cupped his tight balls. He swore they were as hard as his cock.

The bed sagged as she sat, bouncing him lightly against her palm.

"Easy please," he panted. "I'd love to come in your mouth or joined together."

Bunny rose to her knees, giving him a quick wink. Her head bobbed toward him. Her hot breath rushed over him. "I'll see what I can do."

Tight wetness swallowed him. Fast flicks of tongue and lips inched him higher and closer to the edge. Intense waves of pleasure erupted deep in his belly. If his hands were unbound, he would have held her firmly in place, working his aching shaft in and out of her heated mouth. Instead, restrained and restricted in movement, he jerked his hips each time she deep-throated him.

"Best make your decision soon," he groaned out through clenched teeth.

Her head rose, releasing him with a mute pop from her puckered lips. Her excited scent wafted over him with each grabbed breath. Her hands continued stroking and fondling him. "Much more and I'm gonna come."

He moaned as her hand slid up his shaft, capturing him in a brief squeeze of her fist. She let go and worked her way to the foot of the bed, stopping to mouth each testicle before rising.

"You've been a good toy. Mutual pleasure presents such exquisite possibilities."

She plucked two of the condoms from the table, tossing them on his chest. He groaned, eyeing their textures. French tickler or ribbed studs inside and out. What wicked pleasures did she have in mind?

Tapping her chin, she appeared in thought. "I'd say you choose. But..." She licked her lips.

Had he unleashed a wanton? If he didn't come soon, her next touch would find a surprise she hadn't planned on.

Sliding the condoms off him, she stretched out beside him, and her turned palm upward. "You decide which condom. I decide which position."

Brent inhaled sharply. He didn't think he could take the friction and heated sensations the double studded offered. Perhaps another time. The French tickler would rub her g-spot, producing what he hoped would be a double blow for her.

"Tickler," he rasped out, her hand fondling his extremely sensitive tip. At least wearing the condom would reduce direct stimulation. Biting his lip, he glanced at her. Bunny's lurid smirk said her mind percolated. Where had her imagination run now?

Licking his lips, he inhaled, preparing to question his fate. She beat him to it. "Wondering what's next?"

Bunny strolled her fingers down his ticklish side, making him jerk. Tossing the unchosen condom on the wheel chair's seat, she rolled to her knees. "You're very close, aren't you?"

"Yes," he growled. She held him close to his groin.

"Poor baby," she whispered, her mouth inches above him.

Tendrils of her breath pushed him as he teetered along the edge. Once he blew, he was out for the count. He jumped, almost bending in half at her light kiss and lick. There wouldn't be a double for him tonight.

* * * *

Grasping him firmly, Bunny worked the condom down and over him. She moved as quickly as she dared. Straddling him, she rocked forward, rubbing her engorged clit against him. Their combined vocals heated the air.

Reaching between them, she positioned Brent. Her other hand untied the scarf binding his wrists. She sat back, taking him deep within her.

His hands sought her hips. "No," she gasped, her muscles contracting and milking him. "Together please," she blurted out, pulling one of his hands to her breasts and the other to her clit.

Brent rocked his hips in and out slowly at first. She constricted and tightened on each outward stroke. His thumb alternated caresses on her clit. He pulled and plucked her nipple in time to their increasing rhythm.

Brent's contorted expressions and gasps spoke of his impending release. Using her hands and forearms to steady her swaying, she gave him more range of motion. His hips moved faster, plunging the tickler several times across her G-spot in rapid succession. Her own short pants told of her rapid approach.

"How close?" he spat out, his eyes meeting hers.

"Now," she cried, her eyes locked with his.

He tugged her to him, capturing her lips. Their mutual pleasured outbursts muffled between them. Small moans and low-pitched groans spilled out as they both found release.

* * * *

Several moments passed while they rocked with their bodies' lessening need. As quiet enveloped them, Brent rolled Bunny to his side. Her pants echoed his. Gulping air, he closed his eyes. Sleep threatened to claim him. Raising his head, he cracked one eye and nudged her. "Untie me please?"

Her soft giggles made him smile. "Yeah, give me a moment. I think my body's around here somewhere." She breathed deeply. She'd obviously been blown away, too. There'd be time to compare notes later.

He propped himself on his elbow and watched her loosening his remaining restraints. She tossed them toward the chair. Inching his way up the bed, he turned on his side. He blew out the Sterno can and dropped the used condom in the trash.

Bunny popped the top sheet and thermal blanket up like a parachute over the bed. They covered all but the top of Brent's head.

Bunny wormed her way beneath the bedding, whispering, "Where's Brent?"

* * * *

Goose bumps broke out on her arms and shoulders. She tugged on the blanket, hoping to wrap up in it. It wouldn't move. She inched closer to Brent, thinking his quiet indicated he slept. Lifting the blanket, she looked underneath and squealed.

Two eyes peered back coupled with an impish smile. "Brent!" she exclaimed as he lowered the covers. "You're gonna pay for that."

"Oh? Thought I already had." His grin along with his arched eyebrows and rolling eyes sent her into fits of laughter.

"Brent," she gasped, laughing harder as he tickled her in earnest. "Stop! Behave!"

"Make me," he teased, renewing his assault.

"Okay , you asked for it." She turned pulling her legs up and slid them toward him.

"God bless, woman!" Brent called out. "Your feet are like ice. Get 'em off me."

"Stop tickling."

"Not until you move your ice cakes."

Deciding to go for it, her cold hands grasped him. Pay dirt! His sharply gasped "Damn" made her grin.

"Woman, get beneath these blankets now." Brent pulled her closer, cocooning them in the bed's warmth. Chafing her hands with his, he urged her nearer. Her head settled on his shoulder as she snuggled next to him. Her soft breathing blew across his neck. Glancing at her, he smiled. Her lips curled in a soft smile as she closed her eyes.

Bunny watched Brent fight to keep his eyes open. Turning his head to her, he mumbled, "Good night, my love. Love you."

Bunny's eyes flew open. Brent's chest rose and fell under her hand. His soft snores confirmed he slept. Had he really said it? My love and love you?

Should she jolt him awake and demand confirmation? Avoid the issue? Ignore it? Sleep threatened to claim her. She needed to move to her bed. She wasn't ready for Kate to find them together yet.

Lifting her hand, she inched away. A sense of loneliness enveloped her. Her sleep-fogged brain dragged her deeper into a semi-conscious state, half awake, half dreaming. Images formed behind her closed eyes. In one, she explained to Kate about Brent. Another found her telling Phillip to mind his own business. The most vivid sat her straight up. Half awake, she glanced around the room. No Kate! Thanks goodness! Brent turned over, exposing the nightstand clock.

Bunny slid to the edge of the bed. Chills raced across her arms as she gathered her clothes and tiptoed out the door. Six hours until morning. Glad for the cover of night, she hurried to her room. She snuggled into her down comforter's warmth, bereft of human companionship. She'd felt lonelier as of late without Brent beside her each night. Had she'd gotten used to him and his presence?

Her heart thumped an extra beat as she remembered their evening's fun. Part of her wanted to crawl back into his bed, Kate's reaction be dammed. Another section warned against it. A smothered yawn quieted further deliberations. Her last coherent thought made her smile. She cared for him, and it didn't scare her.

* * * *

Brent yawned and stretched. Sunlight streamed through the partly closed blinds. Beams pierced his eyes each time he moved. If he had to stay longer, he'd ask about moving the bed or putting up black-out drapes. Shading his eyes, he checked the time, eight-thirty a.m. He jolted upright and turned.

"Bunny," he called, reaching toward her as more light blinded him.

His hand dropped to the mattress and bounced. Cold met his hand. Squinting, he peered at the open space beside him. She'd left in the night. Despite their agreement to keep things circumspect due to Kate, his heart's forlorn beat echoed louder than before.

Snippets of the previous night rolled across his mind as he scooted to the edge of the bed. He smelled chocolate each time he inhaled. The fondue pot and brushes lay where they'd landed in their haste to couple. Brent grinned as two brightly colored scarves came into view.

Last night had been hot, passionate, and thorough, taking its toll on each of them. Bunny's double orgasm coupled with his delayed release left them wrung out and sleep ready.

With Bunny, a peaceful lull filled him. Warm, soft, feminine flesh spooned near or against him eased the emptiness he felt without her around. He saw things differently. It was as if she complemented who he was and accepted him. He was...*content*. Chuckling, he pulled the wheelchair to him. He tossed the scarves and unused condom on the bed. Whistling, he wheeled toward the bathroom. When he found her, he hoped she was alone. He planned on hugging and kissing her good morning.

* * * *

Bunny returned Kate's wave and smile as she and Max pulled away. Sighing, Bunny turned back to the table holding a stack of papers Kate had been enthusiastically discussing.

Her baby, all grown up, discussed college. The next moment she'd pushed forms across the table, stating she needed *Mom's* signature.

Ben moved from the short-order grill behind the counter toward the kitchen. He stopped, clearing his throat. Bunny faced him. "Ms. Bunny, we did a good job. You raised her up and put a good head on her shoulders. I taught her self-defense and cooking." He grinned, nodding.

Bunny smiled weakly. "Ah Ben, it seems the precarious balance between hanging on and letting go that totters more toward Kate becoming her own person. She's got Phillip's grit and Christy's tenacity. A real mix of Derrick and me."

Ben turned and padded into the kitchen. He set about prepping lunch as he sang one of the kids' favorite childhood tunes.

Bunny poured a fresh cup of coffee and slid into the first booth, taking Kate's forms with her. She leafed through the stack, separating them into similar piles.

One held applications to several colleges and universities. A few were in-state with the largest portion for out of state. Bunny smiled, remembering her determination to flee home and be out on her own. Kate was better prepared. Still, Bunny didn't know if she was ready. She signed and dated every highlighted line. Thanks to Kate's organization, it took less time than expected.

The second pile held the vast multi-paged financial-aid forms, again yellowed where she needed to sign her name. Bunny chuckled at the color coordinated post-it notes instruction list attached to each set of forms. Kate and her thoroughness. The girl had an eye for detail.

The last pile contained miscellaneous release forms and insurance documents. Different hued tags adorned this batch. Two bright purple tabs drew Bunny's gaze. Pulling them from the stack, she noticed the large binder clip holding them together along with a note from Kate.

Mom,

We've always been upfront with each other. These forms talk about something you don't know…

Bunny's hand shook as she gripped her coffee cup. Raising it, she sloshed warm liquid over her fingers. "Oh Kate," she moaned, dropping her cup.

* * * *

"Morning Ben," Brent called out. "Too late for a short stack?"

"No. Coming right up. Bacon, too?"

"Yes, extra crispy and a couple of eggs. Have you see Bunny?"

"Out front." Ben nodded toward the open kitchen door.

The loud crash of china splintering and silverware clattering poured through the kitchen doorway. Brent and Ben hurried toward the sound.

Ben stopped short of the doorway, moving sideways to allow Brent room to go first. Grabbing the chair's handles, he helped Brent over the slight dip into the dining room. "Thanks," Brent hastily replied and rolled to where Bunny sat sopping up coffee with several napkins.

"Are you all right ? What happened?" Brent asked, checking for signs of injury.

"Yes." Her trembling hands suggested otherwise.

"Clumsy me." Bunny reached for the wad of paper towels Ben offered.

Brent grasped her wrist, steadying it. His thumb rubbed along the underside of her wrist, catching her erratic pulse. Medical training boiled to the top along with an overwhelming rush to pull her into his arms and comfort her. Her paleness and ragged breaths added up to more than clumsiness. Something was up.

"Ben, do you need help?" Brent asked, watching Bunny fidget with the papers before her.

"No. Couple swipes with a broom and mop will finish it up."

"Okay, Bunny and I will be in her office. Call when my breakfast is ready."

Tugging on Bunny's hand, he pulled her to him. She hesitated, her fingers lingering on the papers closest to her. "Bring them and come on."

"What do you think you're doing?" Her forced, edgy tone added to his growing suspicions

"Getting us and these," he picked up one of the stacks, "out of Ben's way."

Ben nodded in agreement. "Go on, Ms. Bunny. It'll take a few moments to finish up. 'Sides, Mr. Brent's breakfast needs to cook." Ben stepped back, giving Brent room to turn.

Dragging another set of papers to him, he plopped the first on his lap and added the second on top. "Ready?" His tone was as clipped as hers. He wheeled forward, expecting her to follow.

Silence filled the space between them. Ben decided against valor and to retreat into the kitchen. He had a broom and mop to retrieve. Before his hasty departure, he helped Bunny to her feet and whispered. "Let 'em help. He's a good man." Bunny's glare quieted his further response.

Chapter Twelve

Brent wheeled in the office first, making room for her. Bunny made sure the door closed behind them.

How dare he! How dare he—dare he what? Her heart prompted. *Care? Step up, be there, and help?* Damn it, she didn't need taking care of. A sick feeling thudded through her sinking heart.

Sweat swept across her palms. The hair on the back of her neck rose, bristling. Her jaw ached. "Blast," she mouthed. She'd done it again. Fear and anxiety gripped her gut. The cycle was starting.

Brent moved aside, letting her past him. She slapped her papers on top of the two stacks already on her desk. Pulling out her chair, she slumped into it. Anger reared its ugly head, flaring her flight mechanism into being. She swore her wet palms left marks on her pants as she rubbed them along her legs. Vowing to not back down, she raised her eyes to his.

Brent returned her glare. His arms folded tight across his chest worried her more. Her heart dropped lower. Derrick had continuously shut her out when he took over. Ice-cold chills rushed up her back. A fight was coming. Brent's set jaw belied his resolve.

Bunny gulped and pushed herself upright in her chair. Best thing was to get it over with and out in the open. She didn't like feeling shut out and at odds with someone she cared about. Kate's revelation had shaken her enough.

A pregnant pause welled up between them. Seconds clicked off the wall clock, each tick louder than the last. Bunny counted and waited. Thirty ticks later, he moved. Good. She was tired of his cat and mouse tactics.

"What are these?" Brent asked, tapping the papers between them.

"Forms Kate needs my signature on." She wasn't saying more.

"I can see that. Since when does signing your name make you cry out?" His gaze locked with hers. Although his arms were still crossed, they sat looser on his chest.

She inhaled, counting to five and exhaled. Perhaps the rigidness in his shoulders had disappeared. Okay, maybe he wasn't as angry as she suspected.

"It's something I can handle. Don't worry." She blinked and tried to smile.

Brent smacked his hand on the desk. "Damn it, Bunny! Don't shut down on me."

Two distinct memories flashed through her mind. Her similar reaction to Derrick's refusal to talk about his work-related stress and ambitious overdrive. And, Amy's admonishment about letting her guard down and letting people in. When had she walled up her heart? Locked herself away and tossed out the keys? Wetting her lips, she leaned forward.

"Brent, I'm not keeping you out. I'm playing it safe." There, she said it. Acid rose like volcanic lava, burning her hard-won peace. Her damn stomach flip-flopped like a thousand butterflies fought to escape. Risk. The one thing she vowed never to overdo again. She teetered on the edge of repeating it again.

* * * *

Brent pulled the papers to him. He wanted to help. Marta wouldn't let him. She'd refused to accept more than she felt comfortable with. She hadn't wanted to be beholding to anyone. He raised his head. Marta had her limits. So did Bunny. He'd follow his heart better this time.

"I'm not sure why you're doing that. I want to help where I can."

A hard knock and the door opening drew their attention. Ben entered, carrying Brent's breakfast. "I fixed your coffee black with a little sugar and buttered the pancakes. Syrup is in the small bowl. I'll be back with your eggs in a few." He hastily departed.

Brent lifted the plate covering his pancakes and bacon. He sighed. Could Ben read minds? Ben had taken over and done for him what he could have done for himself. Yet Ben's actions had made his job easier. Ben hadn't intentionally sugared the coffee and buttered the pancakes because Brent couldn't.

"No, you want to fix it. Do it for me." Bunny's accusation hit home. Her sarcastic tone cut to his core. Why couldn't she leave well enough alone and let him... *Let you what? Take over? Do it for her?* Damn his conscience. Why did it need to sound like a cross between Marta and Bunny? *Well?* Okay, he got the point.

"Let me—"

"Eat your breakfast and hear me out."

He nodded and shrugged. Ben's quick in and out with his eggs and coffee for Bunny left him no choice.

Bunny looked at him oddly as she creamed and sugared her coffee. He kept silent and began eating.

* * * *

Clearing a space between them, Bunny separated the stacks. "I don't normally share family matters in any detail. If I need help, I ask only for what I specifically need."

Brent's raised eyebrows told her she had his attention. He continued chewing, offering no input.

"Since this indirectly involves you and Kate, I will explain part of it." His eyes widened, yet he remained quiet.

Bunny paused, her hackles ready. A rapid retort lay on her tongue, ready to spew forth. Brent stumped her. He said nothing and motioned for her to continue. *Hmmm, a male who actually listened?*

"This stack," she pushed the nearest pile to him closer, "is college applications. Thanks to your help and persistence, Kate's grade point rose to widen the number of colleges that would accept her. Thank you."

"You're welcome." He went back to eating. He gestured with his fork, pointing to the pile midway between them.

Oh, he was playing it up. Her hackles bustled, and acid dripped down her throat. Two could play the game. She picked up her coffee and began sipping while leafing through the appointed stack. She dropped her gaze, glancing slightly every few seconds at him.

His jaw moved with forced tightness. He chewed with exaggerated motion. She nibbled her lip to keep from grinning. She'd gotten to him. Why didn't it feel good? Her stomach gurgled and flopped each time his teeth clenched and jaw moved.

'Cuz you care, and his reaction matters. Crap, that again. Bunny drummed her fingers on the desktop and spoke.

"Financial-aid papers and release forms for the bank to send out personal and business statements."

"I see." His simple, cold-toned reply frosted her more. Chills reached deeper into her. Not even two quick swallows of coffee staved them off. She wrapped her arms around her middle and alternately chafed her arms.

"Something wrong?" he asked, stressing each word and adding emphasis with his arched eyebrow.

When had he gotten this close? Close enough for her to let her guard down so far, open her tightly locked vault of feelings, and let him in. She shook inside at her realization.

Inserting her hands under her folded arms, she tried staring back. Acute fear leaped through her when he just sat there and watched. His stoic stubbornness scared her. Yet, a quiet whisper resounded deep in her heart. *He ain't walking, so start talking.* She sighed and asked the question pestering her most. "Why?"

"Why what?" he responded, leaning forward, his voice less harsh.

"Why do you want to help? Why get involved?" Her hands shook harder as she unfolded her arms.

Brent must have seen her unease. He offered his hand palm up to her.

"Because I care. Kate is important like you are. I help people I care about. Friends, co-workers, and lo—" He stopped speaking. His hand touched hers.

While he spoke, she'd risked putting her hand near his. She jumped at his touch.

* * * *

Brent ran his thumb lightly across Bunny's knuckles. Her pulse sped up and became jittery with each rub. Something had her spooked. She licked her lips, and her pulled-taunt mouth told him more than she realized.

"Why does my helping bother you?" He loosened his hold on her hand and ceased thumbing her knuckles. He hoped his tone and pitch projected calm and sincerity. His heart skipped a few beats at the tears he saw her blink away.

Crap! Tears, his one ultra-vulnerable button. Brent inhaled deeply and exhaled slowly. He fought against his ingrained parental teachings about acquiescing when his sisters cried. His heart was in this and their future. Could he remain neutral?

"Helping is one thing," Bunny began, her voice garbled by her repressed sobs. "Taking over is another."

Brent counted to three and spoke. "Did Derrick and others take over rather than help?"

Bunny's silent nod said a lot.

"Go on," he encouraged.

"Kate is my daughter. I welcome input and suggestions. Telling me what to do or how to do it isn't acceptable."

"I see. So this is about the way I stepped up or how I said things. Right?"

"That's part of it." Maybe the boulder between them was about to disappear.

"And the other?"

* * * *

Did she dare come right out and say the word? How big a battle was she prepared to wage? Tremors renewed their erratic beat from her heart to her stomach and back. How well did she know her own feelings? Maybe subtlety was a better tactic.

"And what's the other part?"

She hoped he continued along his current train of thought about how he stepped up and how he'd spoken. Moving her hands off the desk, she fidgeted with a raveling hanging from her shirtsleeve just below the desk edge.

"I appreciate your candor. But your reluctance to share with me, or even discuss the issue as much as we have talked about, troubles me. The other part I'm talking about is why we had to fight about it in the first place"

A pent-up sigh threatened to escape. Her growing frustration and lack of words to solidify her thoughts and feelings frightened her. Last time she'd been this anxious and worried, she'd been falling in love with Derrick. Fear etched its icy claws up her spine, seeking to freeze out any rational action.

"I'm sorry you're troubled. How would you feel if someone took over making decisions for you or tried to help without asking how or if you needed or wanted it?"

Brent's quiet and mindful expression impressed her. He appeared to be weighing her question and thinking about his answer. Regardless of her present feelings and concerns, he garnered a few more brownie points for this.

"You know, as I think about it, I can relate from personal experience."

"Oh?" A thought rushed across her mind. Had she done that to him?

"Yeah, Amy did it when she first came over. I chewed her out for it. Tom tried to help and ended up being overly problematic 'cuz he didn't ask, just did. Today, Ben did it inadvertently, making his job easier, but he didn't ask before doing."

"And?" She wanted his answer before saying more. He seemed to understand her concern. Still, he was male and thought like one nonetheless.

"I reacted and did. I complicated things by jumping into stuff that may not even concern me."

"You've summarized it pretty well. Sometimes you can't ask, you just have to do given circumstances and potential hazardous outcomes."

* * * *

Brent tapped the last stack of papers. "I get the impression this is pretty personal stuff. " He flicked his eyes to Bunny's, waiting her response or a sign he was correct. Her slight nod said he was.

"Can you or do you care to share what's got you upset? I'm here for you. You're not alone."

Her nostrils flared at his last words. Another sensitive button. He'd wanted to punch Derrick and a few other men from her past for acting like jackasses. Braying and drawing attention to themselves without thinking about others. Selfish bastards! Yep, he ranked in that crowd from time to time, too.

Again, tears sparkled in her eyes. Christ, he hated making any woman cry. But someone he loved, well, that put him in his own personal hell. Taking two sharp breaths, he placed both hands palms down on the desk and spoke. "What do you want to share?"

He kept reminding himself to breathe deeply and frequently while she shuffled through the third stack, pulling out a set of purple-tabbed forms. He recognized the author's script. Kate.

Bunny shoved the papers to him. "Remember, I'm not asking you to fix it. I'm sharing." He nodded his understanding and began reading.

...about. Yes, I should have told you. If I had, you would have known.

I wasn't sure I was ready. You taught me to make my own decisions and be myself.

Max and I are having sex. Before you freak, I'm using birth control. Christy took me to Dr. Shapiro on my birthday for a full physical and protection discussion.

Please don't be angry. One of the release forms requires your signature to release all medical history to the school's clinic. My GYN doctor is listed there.

Love,

Kate

Brent lifted his head. His eyes refocused on a growing white pile of shredded napkins in front of Bunny. A good sign. She wasn't stifling her emotions. Taking her hand, he spoke. "Stop. Talk to me, please."

A watery sigh escaped as she answered. "My baby. My youngest is a woman. Part of me wants to hug her for being safe and levelheaded. Then I want to ground her for not coming to me about this." She grabbed a piece of napkin and dabbed her eyes.

"You're pissed off with Christy?"

"Oh, yeah." Bunny's weak grin tugged at his restrained heart. He needed to hold and comfort her. His arms ached to embrace her and share her burden. Damn it, he loved her, and there wasn't a freaking thing he could do to show it.

"Sweetie," he began, reaching for her other hand, "how are you going to handle this?"

"I'm not sure. One thing I know is the past can't be changed. I learned that when Derrick died."

"You're not alone. I'm here and love—"

Bunny's hand shot up. "Stop! Please don't use that word lightly."

"What word?"

"Love."

"Huh? I don't get it."

"L-o-v-e. Don't say what you can't or don't mean. It's not necessary. Sex isn't going to stop because it's not in the equation."

Brent wished he could walk around the desk and throw her over his knee. She needed a spanking. Little did she know how childish she was herself. Pulling the napkin shreds to him, he started ripping them into smaller pieces and counting out loud. "One—two—three—"

"What's that for?" Bunny pointed to the growing mess in front of him.

"Five—six—seven." He stopped and looked at her. "It's either this or we start fighting again." He swept the smaller shards into his hand and dumped them in the wastebasket.

"What are you upset about?" Bunny's question sparked a huge flame of frustration and angst. Did he need to spell it out? Get detailed? God, the woman had a stubborn streak. It was like their gender roles were reversed.

That was it! The answer he'd been looking for. Shoving the papers aside, he grabbed her hand, scattering bits of napkin in the air. Time she answered his questions.

"Look at me," he said, his tone even and quiet. She kept her eyes down. Wrapping his fingers around her wrist, he tugged, stating it again. She glanced up. "Why does it bother you?"

"I don't need the word to go to bed with you." Her eyes lowered.

"I didn't ask that. Why does my loving you bother you?"

He tightened his hold as she tried to free her wrist. Beads of sweat wet his fingers. He could feel her palm getting wetter. Her flaring nostrils showed her distress. But why? What had her spooked? Why wouldn't she share? He couldn't begin to fix—no that was comprehend—if she refused to talk.

He let go of her hand and laid his on hers. "Give it to me straight. I want to understand."

Her pulse threaded beneath his thumb. Each heartbeat thumped her anxiety. He blessed his psychological training. Being able to recognize her fear helped temper his words and actions. Now if he could keep his macho id in check, he might learn a thing or two and keep communication flowing.

Her deep inhalation and lips rubbing together drew his attention. Was she ready? Would she give him what he sought? Or cut him off? He hoped for the former and prayed against the latter.

"I'm not ready to hear it."

Brent waited. Was there more? Her further hesitation didn't do his gut much good. His shortening patience might make him lose what composure he had. Clearing his throat, he turned to face her, leaning more on the desk. Her whispered words made him draw back.

"Men use love to get what they want. Some women wrap up in the word, hoping to cloak themselves in some sort of magical energy that is supposed to solve everything. I don't want to be that woman again. Nor do you need to say it to get what you want."

"What is it that you think I'm wanting when I say it?" He reviewed the times he remembered saying he loved her. How many times had she heard it and under what circumstances?

"Sex."

Her answer rocked him back in his chair.

"Please explain." He wanted to say more but decided against it. What she had to say was important to her.

"Well, given the only time you said it or alluded to it was during or after the act, I figured you were saying or using it to get more. I refuse to believe that it means more. I've become more pragmatic and practical over the years."

"Over the years?" Lord, how jaded and hardened had she become? And for how long?

"Since Derrick's death and I tried dating again."

He clenched his fist as it rested against his leg. *Excuse me on this one*, he prayed, *but Derrick was a real jerk!* If the man had walked into the room, he'd found himself lying on the floor nursing a black eye and sore jaw. What other fools had she ended up passing time with? At least now he had an idea what he was up against. Problem was did he have enough patience and fortitude to battle his own frustrations and stay the course on both his issues as well as hers?

"I enjoy our sexual intimacy. I love you regardless. It's okay you're not ready to hear it."

Chapter Thirteen

Bunny sat with her chin cupped in her hands, paying no attention to who passed Kater's front window. It appeared as though she people-watched. Her mind and thoughts were elsewhere.

Two weeks prior, she'd found out Kate was no longer a virgin. Her oldest daughter had lied to her—correction, omitted telling her about taking her sister to a doctor, her son called to say he was coming for a visit along with his sister, and Brent openly declared he loved her. Nothing much to worry about in the normal course of the world. Wrong!

Kate's attempts to discuss her revelation were met with talk-to-the-hand signals. Bunny didn't think she'd ever be ready to talk about birth control with her youngest. Somehow she had to, and that wasn't the only priority running through her mind. Today was Brent's follow-up appointment with his orthopedist and consultation with the specialist. He refused to let her go along, something about not getting her too involved at this point. She hated not knowing what was going on in her own household. Inside she giggled. The maniacal laugh scared her silly. Brent was part of her and her life whether she was ready to admit it or not.

Ben approached. A fresh pot of coffee in hand, he noisily set a cup on the table and poured. "Ms. Bunny, I know this isn't what you want to hear, but sitting here and waiting for Mr. Brent to return is not doing you any good. Please eat some breakfast, and stop taking the world on your shoulders."

"I suppose you're right, Ben. My stomach refuses to cease making protest noises, and that coffee smells divine. I'll take a cup and some cinnamon swirl French toast sticks."

Ben started toward the kitchen and came back. "You know, Ms. Bunny, I miss Mr. Brent singing as he helps me clear tables and fill the dishwasher. Even Ms. Kate has been quiet."

"I miss Brent's singing, too." Bunny reached for the cream pitcher. "Things have been quieter around here."

"I wish we'd go back to being like a family. You know, trusting each other and talking. Not blaming or ignoring like some folks think families do. Lord knows we care for and need each other." Ben smiled and entered the kitchen.

Bunny sat the cream pitcher down and picked up her spoon. She stirred her coffee as she sugared it. She sadly smiled. She remembered waiting for Kate to come home from school during her elementary years. In a few short months, she would be graduating and going off to college. Where had the time flown? It seemed like yesterday she'd come home with her first report card and pig tails bobbing as she ran in the front door. A noise drew her from her thoughts.

Bunny looked up. Ben stood behind Kate. "Ms. Bunny, I didn't know Ms. Kate was here." He approached the table, her French toast in one hand, the other holding her silverware and napkin.

"It's alright Ben. Go ahead and put it down. Kate, do you want some breakfast or coffee?"

Kate slid into the booth opposite her. "Yes to both. Ben, add some sausage to the French toast, please."

Ben shrugged after he set Bunny's plate in front of her and walked away, shaking his head.

Ben's last departure after serving Kate's food ended noisily as he muttered, carrying the breakfast rush's dirty dishes to the kitchen. Several moments of silence passed.

* * * *

Kate snuck a glance at her mother. A soft grin quirked Kate's lips. Ben didn't lose his cool often. His temper was boiling if she'd caught his few understandable words right.

"Mom," she began, catching Bunny with her mouth full. "Yes, I am cutting classes, and I know you're not happy about it. But we need to talk."

Bunny's slight nod encouraged her to continue.

"I didn't make a good choice." Kate paused, waiting for her mother's reaction. Bunny's eyes snapped to hers.

"I should have come to you like Christy suggested, and we could have talked it out."

"Yes, that would have saved some grief. Why didn't you?"

"Because you'd discourage me. Say I'm too young." Kate hesitated before adding her final statement. "The same age you were when you and Daddy did it."

Bunny's furled eyebrow and narrowed eyes made Kate gulp. She bit into a French toast stick and chewed.

* * * *

Bunny resisted yelling and setting her cup down hard. The girl had Derrick's determination and his uncanny ability to push buttons. What was it Brent had said? *Let your emotions out. Just keep 'em leashed.* She smiled at his advice. Looking at Kate, she noticed her eating with gusto. *Keep your mouth full, girl. Momma is gonna speak.*

"Kate, you're going to be nineteen soon and off to college. I want the best for you just like I did and do for Phillip and Christy."

Kate nodded.

"Your dad and I learned about choice after Christy was on the way. We got married because we wanted to. If we'd waited and gotten better information, things might have turned out differently.

Kate's wide-eyed stare made Bunny stop. Time for a frank discussion had come.

"Your dad quit school to get a fulltime job. He didn't resent being a father. I continued my classes until Christy was born. Grandma and Grandpa were paying for mine."

"Daddy never finished?" Kate's question triggered Derrick's nasty remarks from deep in Bunny's memories. Folding her hands together tightly, she answered.

"He graduated several years later after Phillip was born. His job paid for him to go. He'd taken a job as an emergency dispatcher."

Kate placed her empty plate atop hers. "Are you saying Daddy wasn't happy?"

How did she tell Kate the truth? That her father resented her mother's achievements and had become driven and goal-obsessed to earn more than her and get a better job. He'd become jealous of her finishing her desired degree and landing a job making more than he did. It hadn't helped that her parents paid for her to finish her education.

"Dad loved each of you in his own way. His determination and drive blinded him in the end. He wanted the best and decided he alone could do it for us."

Bunny grew silent, her thoughts rolling back over the years. Good times mixed with the bad helped to ease the darker, bleaker moments. Would she and Derrick still be married? Did they have what it would have taken for the long haul? Hindsight showed probably not. That wasn't for Kate to know.

"Mom," Kate started and blinked back tears, "I'm sorry."

"It's okay. I'm your mom and love you no matter what."

"I know." Kate grinned. "You've put up with some real crazy stuff over the years."

Bunny smiled and emptied her cup. "Now, Miss Skipping Classes, what else is up?"

Kate rummaged in her discarded jacket pocket. "I got this from my guidance counselor when I got to school." She smoothed out the envelope and handed it to Bunny. The return address read Richboro College, Richboro, North Carolina.

Accepting the envelope, Bunny opened it. She scanned the first few lines. "What do you know about this?" she asked, looking up.

Kate sat taller and straighter. A huge smile lit up her face. "Remember the two-day away game tournament a few months back?"

"The one with Richboro High? Yes."

"Ms. Warren arranged a tour of Richboro College for us. I talked to their admissions office and showed them my S.A.T. scores since we'd just gotten them."

"You came back sounding disinterested in them."

"Since I decided to double major in finance and business, and they didn't offer both, yeah. That was until I got this." Kate pointed excitedly at the letter.

Bunny read further.

Ms. Kate Kater, we would like to welcome you to Richboro College's Class of 2012.

Our new dual degree program allows interested candidates, such as you, the opportunity to combine curriculums and earn two degrees at once. Your grade point average and S.A.T. scores indicate you have what it takes to succeed in this complex program. As one of the first twenty students entering the program, we are pleased to offer you a full scholarship covering all costs for four years.

Bunny folded the letter and placed it on the table. Lacing her fingers together, she searched Kate's face. Kate's eyes darted back and forth from the letter to her. Did the girl want to go? What were her thoughts? "Kate, what do you think?"

The tip of Kate's tongue slipped between her lips. A glowing spark lit her eyes. Bunny felt her heart skip a beat. Her last chick would soon be gone.

"Mom, it wouldn't cost us much at all. Possibly incidentals. We've talked about how much school you could afford and how much better immersing myself in my studies full-time would be."

"Are you sure? We just sent out the other applications. What did Ms. Warren say?"

"A tentative interest will hold my place until March with a definitive yes or no needed by June. I have time to consider other options and schools." Kate reached across the table and squeezed Bunny's hand. "Mom, someday soon, I'm going to be leaving. I'm glad you've got Brent."

Kate carried their dishes to the kitchen. A low-keyed conversation between her and Ben flowed out to Bunny. Two quick laughs drew her from her ponderings.

"Mom," Kate stopped near her, "Ben says he wants to add his name to my list of first clients when I open my accounting firm."

Bunny smiled, though her mind rattled with rushing ideas and partly formed images.

Kate hugged her and whispered, "Mom, don't worry. I'll be okay."

Patting Kate's arm, she blinked back tears. Her baby was moving on. "I'm sure you will, honey. It's just a bit of a shock. It'll take some adjustment to being alone."

"Alone? Mom, what about Brent?"

Bunny stood and slipped her arm around Kate's waist. "Come in the office so I can write you that note to get back into school. I'll run you back on my way to do errands."

* * * *

"Ouch!" Brent yelled. "That hurts."

The physical therapist smiled and nodded. Brent eyed her wryly.

"Mr. Stephens, Dr. Standford wants a mobility report while he waits for the full x-ray results. Now flex your knee and toes again please."

Brent scowled and grimaced as he bent his leg and pressed against the floor with his toes. His now bare limb echoed the whiteness of the cast that formerly covered it. It hurt to move and yet felt so good. The ironical side of his sense of humor kicked in as he remembered the lyrics from a Queen song. "*Ooh, ooh pain is so close to pleasure.*"

The physical therapist scribbled notes in his chart after observing his movement for several minutes. "All right, let's get you over to casting."

"What?" Brent yelped, gripping the arms of his wheelchair.

"Dr. Sanders is meeting us there."

Brent nodded, keeping his curse words and mutterings sub-vocal. The specialist would be with Sanders. Brent switched his thoughts to praying, hoping the surgeon wasn't next.

The physical therapist wheeled Brent back to casting where Dr. Sanders and the specialist were viewing his x-rays.

"Mr. Stephens," the specialist looked at Brent's chart and glanced to the x-ray viewer, "you are one lucky man. A compound fracture or a sprain can put you out of commission. Both together can be disastrous." Setting down the chart, he had Brent press against his hand and wriggle his toes. As Brent flexed and moved, he slid his hands carefully up and down Brent's calf and ankle.

Brent sat quiet, his heart racing and skipping beats. The specialist wrote rapidly in his chart. What was next? Much more of this blasted wheelchair and he'd go nuts. Sounds of a throat clearing drew him back to the present.

"I've ordered an MRI to be sure there's no extensive damage. Depending on what it shows, I'm ordering a new lightweight cast either with a walker or support boot."

Brent wanted to sing and dance. Dance...how long had it been since he'd held a woman close, cherishing and cradling her against him as they swayed to a slow love song? His and Marta's wedding and at Bunny's birthday party. He and Bunny were overdue. Rubbing his hands together, he planned for when and where they would.

* * * *

Bunny sat waiting for the light to change. In her rearview mirror, she watched as Kate and Max stood holding hands and talking. Senior days granted graduating students privileges. In a few hours, Kate would be home and off with her friends studying for finals. In a few more months, her baby would be out of high school and on her way to college. Where had the time gone?

Bunny shook her head and turned the corner. Kate's parting remarks echoed through her mind. "You're not alone. Brent will be with you. He's different, isn't he?"

Single...unpaired...no one. Regardless how many ways she reworded it, tried redefining it or changing views, she'd be on her own. The empty nest was coming. How much longer would Brent be around? Sure, he'd be there until he lost the wheelchair. Today could be it.

She needed to prepare for what was coming. What could she really prepare for? Changes were happening. And even more could come. Seeing friends took only a couple hours a week. Amy's free time had dwindled since her return to work and promotion.

Ben had begun shooing her out of the kitchen since off-season started. Most days he handled both breakfast and lunch rushes.

Bunny parked her car and watched the people milling around her. A couple walked by holding hands. A mother smiled and cooed at her toddler seated in the shopping cart holding her purchases. A group of teen girls noisily passed, caught up in their chatter. Male voices called out to them. One or two individuals passed her.

Crap! Bunny smacked her steering wheel. Somewhere along the line, she'd isolated herself. Young and alone, wrapped in her fear and insecurities, she had sought to insulate against risk, dependency, and—

Loss? Her inner voice suggested. Yes, that too as much as she hated to admit it. When had autopilot become normal? Hell, when had anything felt or seemed right? Wariness had become the watchword guarding every action.

Images of Kate and Max holding hands, standing close together, talking animatedly, flashed through her mind. One time, she and Derrick had been like that. Then the joy and newness wore off. She gasped as memories came flooding back.

"Oh God," she murmured. Shortly before she learned she was pregnant with Kate, Derrick mentioned filing for divorce. The papers never arrived due to his death. The fights after Phillip and Christy were asleep that contained the nasty remarks and comments poured forth. Silent tears slipped down her cheeks. Fumbling for a tissue, she cried, holding nothing back. Grief and saying good-bye to the past were long overdue.

Reaching into her purse for another tissue, her hand brushed paper. She wiped her eyes and stared at the folded item. Carefully extracting it, she opened and read the written words.

Bunny,

I want to apologize for being such an ass at times. Loving someone is not always easy. We risk being vulnerable and hurt.

We've each had our share of good and bad times. I'd like to share those with you as your friend or lover. Maybe both. That way neither of us has to be alone again.

I'm game. Are you?

Brent

A smile curled her lips. Being alone didn't hold any appeal. God, she had learned that the hard way over the last year. Kate spent more time immersed in schoolwork or away. Ben left late afternoons or early evening depending on business. Too many nights watching re-runs or curled-up with a book began to add up. How many nights alone could a person take? It wasn't like she was an extreme extrovert or overly introverted. Companionship had merits.

Dating filled a few hours here and there. But finding someone and spending time getting to know them along with the energy bored her after awhile. She got tired of hunting and being hunted.

She snickered at her last thought. Some had stalked her, too, refusing to take no for an answer until they heard about her flattening the heaviest fireman on Brent's staff.

Kate's question pinged again. Was she comparing all men to Derrick? Or some high ideal none would or could measure up to?

Sighing, she didn't like the answer that came to mind. Guilty as charged on both accounts. How he had gotten past those barriers? When had he gotten so close that she wanted to be with him, sought him out and, damn him, made her care?

He's different, unlike the rest. Don't be silly, her heart screamed.

As much as she didn't want to admit it, he was. Neither of them had approached the other with a curiosity beyond neighbors. Her smile grew. Their mutual interest and chemistry had boiled just below the surface. Each had held their desire in-check. She grew warm reviewing their interactions up to their first kiss. Boy, had she been blind. She missed or brushed off the subtle hints and gestures. Yes, the man was different.

Not once had Brent stated or laid an expectation on her. Derrick's had gone unsaid but inserted themselves in every fight, putdown, or nasty comment.

Patience seemed to rule Brent's actions and ethics. And he carried it over to his interactions with Kate. The teeter-totter levered more towards yes. His anger came out, yet he regained composure quickly. Even with his crew, he took time to understand and interact with each, playing up their strengths and encouraging them. Reprimands happened. It was part of his job.

Bunny sighed and nodded. Leave it to Kate. She'd seen what her mother missed. She'd asked what they'd been fighting about after observing their overly polite nature to each other.

The man didn't back down. He drew her in and fought just the same. He wanted to hear and know how she felt. The best was he listened and learned, even to the point of acting upon it. She'd miss him if he left. That was an emptiness she didn't want to face.

Closing her eyes, she searched her mind and worked to quiet her rapid heartbeat. She mouthed the question only she could answer. Did she love him?

Chapter Fourteen

Brent lowered his leg to the exam table and lay back. He took a deep breath, exhaled, and nodded.

A low-grade hum reverberated against the top of his head. Rolling his eyes back, he saw the long cylinder housing the main imaging components moving toward him. Two more passes and he'd know. If patience equaled virtue, well, he was out of both.

Tingles flowed up and down his body. The hair on his arms bristled along with the hair on his head. God, he wanted to scratch and move his leg. The cylinder passed over his stomach.

Dr. Sanders, the specialist, and the surgeon decided on a complete body scan. The surgeon wanted a clear picture of both legs, hips, and tendons. The specialist focused on his ankle and Achilles heel. Dr. Sanders needed their signatures and recommendations for the next phase of treatment. He looked down the cylinder as it rolled back toward his head. Brent closed his eyes and continued breathing deeply.

* * * *

Bunny hummed a jaunty little tune her dad had taught her as a child. She smiled and snorted at the bawdy lyrics she remembered him singing until her mother put a stop to it.

Two more trips and Phillip's room would be ready. Christy's miscellaneous trappings and personal effects sat boxed in her closet. The junk her children refused to part with.

Her nose twitched, and her eyes watered. No more sneezes please, she prayed. Dust and dander filled the air with each stuffed animal she tossed in the box. "Either they take it with them or it goes."

She grinned. Another solid decision made. Her earlier one warmed her heart and loins. She wondered what Brent's response would be.

Tape and scissors sat atop the smallest of the four sealed boxes. Pen in hand, she marked the contents and Phillip's name on each one. Two medium-sized boxes sat empty in the middle of the bed. Brent's belongings would fill those. She pondered their destination. Looking at her watch, she calculated how much longer until she heard from him.

* * * *

Tony's grin grew. Brent returned it. His desk was littered with papers. Get-well cards from various sections of Jameston adorned his office bulletin board and greeted him. Damn, it felt good to be back behind his desk even if it meant limited duty for a while longer. He wasn't ready to share the news with Bunny. He needed a bit more time and space to ascertain his next move in their growing relationship. He hoped the box he asked Randy to send arrived soon. Randy's reaction still rang in his ears. Brent's own caution rumbled through his heart and stomach. Or was that the smell of Tony's chili dogs tantalizing his taste buds?

"Tony, what you got cooking? It smells great."

"Chili con carne y queso. My Hispanic neighbor's killer combination toned down from its five-alarm hotness. Goes great with brauts and fries."

"Any chance of getting some?" Brent pushed back from his desk, ready to wheel into the kitchen.

"Sure, Chief. You stay put. Tom's been nagging me about supplies. He mentioned wanting to talk to you. I'll send him in and bring enough for both of you."

Brent shook his head and slid the stack of papers to him. Seeing Tom's note on top, he wondered if the man had overdone it again. He was always trying a bit too hard.

Twenty minutes later, Brent faced Tom. "Okay, have a seat, and let's talk."

Tom sat next to Brent. "I see you're going through the stuff I left for you."

"Yes, and I want to thank you for taking on my job with yours. It hasn't been easy I'm sure."

"You're welcome. It's not what I thought the job entailed. You were right. I have a lot to learn."

Brent chuckled. He knew Tom frowned on stating his limitations aloud. "Don't sweat it. Our company is well staffed and one of the highest trained in the region. That is why Richmond is increasing our state funds and funding ongoing training for other nearby stations. Seems we are to be emulated and assist them in setting up modules."

Tom's smile and relaxed posture eased the stress holding Brent's shoulders captive. He knew his next statement would get Tom's adrenaline started.

"How do you feel about going to school?"

Tom's eyes widened, and his mouth moved. No words came out.

A knock pounded on the office door. "Come in," Brent called out.

Tony entered and sat two bowls of chili and crackers down. "Two cold root beers coming up. As close to beer as you get for now. Enjoy."

Tom stirred his crackers into his and watched Brent ingest two spoonfuls before he coughed and wiped his eyes. "Maybe we should wait for the root beer?"

"If that is toned down, remind me to put a huge caution sign on that stuff at the cook-off."

Tom took a tentative bite and swallowed. His eyes watered and spasms of coughing threatened to spew forth. Pounding the desk, his mouth dropped open, and he fanned his tongue.

"Yeah, I hope Tony gets back with that root beer real soon! While we're waiting, I want to discuss your request for further training."

Tony left two bottles for each on his return along with frosted glasses. His Cheshire cat grin made both men laugh.

Brent picked up where he'd left off. "Region wants all assistant chiefs qualified in leadership, medical emergency technician standards, and other trauma and triage protocol. What do you think?"

"Sounds like a lot of classroom time. What about field experience? Practical training?"

"That is where you come in. Once you're certified in a couple of areas, your time in the field counts toward a lot of this. The tiers for assistant chief are approved, and with each class, you can opt for more specific training or general education. Either way, you're a top candidate for assistant chief first class. So are you in?"

Tom raised his glass. "Here's to my promotion and further edification."

Clinking glasses with him, Brent nodded. Tom deserved the chance to move up and prove his mettle. He'd stepped in and taken over without issue or hesitation. Brent hoped he remained on staff once he completed his schooling.

* * * *

Bunny placed the last bag of trash in the dumpster. Kate held the door, waiting for her return. Several boxes lined the corridor leading to their living quarters. More cast-offs and unwanted items of useable quality marked for delivery to the thrift store and shelter filled the boxes.

"We'll help," a voice called out. Bunny looked up. Two heads appeared over Kate's shoulder. Steve and Chuck, bless them, stepped over the two smaller boxes propping the door open and lifted the two largest containers. "Where do you want them?"

"In the back of the truck. Thank you."

"No problem." Chuck grinned and winked as he came back, taking the box she held. "Tom asked us to check on you when he saw you hauling stuff out."

Bunny smiled, shaking her head. Still doing penance. Poor Tom seemed he'd never live down his bold cheeky remark two months earlier. Someday she'd have to thank him. It had sparked a change in her and Brent's interactions.

"Chuck, Kate can show you everything that goes in the truck. I appreciate your help."

"You're welcome, Ms. Bunny. Come on, Steve."

Bunny watched as box after box filled the truck. In between each container, she glanced toward the station. Where was Brent? Why hadn't he called?

Steve stopped in front of her. "Ms. Bunny, the chief is talking to Tom and Tony. He said if you asked to let you know he'd talk to you later. He has things to take care of."

Bunny nodded and thanked him. "Come on, Kate. We'll take this over to the shelter and thrift store."

Steve and Chuck hopped in the back of the truck.

"Guys, Mom and I can handle it," Kate blurted out.

Steve held up his hand. "We're to help you dump or deliver it. Do all you need to do to help Ms. Bunny is what Tom said. Let's go."

Kate turned to Bunny. "Mom?"

Bunny shrugged and pulled her keys from her pocket. "Grab my purse, and let's get it done."

Ten minutes later, Bunny parked in the thrift store's rear delivery area. Two store attendants helped Steve and Chuck. Another checked off a detailed list, preparing her donation receipt.

"Ms. Bunny?" Chuck approached, holding her contribution paperwork. "There's a new shelter across town that could use a delivery of clothes and food. The store manager wanted to know if you'd mind making the delivery. It's twenty minutes from the shelter."

What could it hurt? They were headed that direction. Helping others came naturally to her. So many had been there for her when she needed it, paying it back or forward only made sense.

"Sure. Load the clothing and food while I let Ben know we'll be a bit longer."

An air of good cheer and warmth rippled through her heart. Vibrancy filled her. It was as though she'd been sleeping and finally awoken, ready to face life. Except this time, she didn't plan to be alone. She'd take the risk and pray the outcome didn't find her solo. Chills ran down her spine, pooling in her gut. She hesitated, waiting for fear's icy grip to claim its prize.

Nothing—nada, zip, zilch—cooled her sense of calm and peace. Two steps forward and she prayed none backward were waiting for her. A certain someone wanted a frank discussion and stated he'd been waiting for it. Well, she was ready. Was he?

* * * *

Tom laughed as Brent wiped his forehead. "Damn good chili!" He smiled and downed the last of his root beer. "Remind me to take the Tabasco sauce out of the kitchen before Tony makes it again."

He stood, gathering his dishes. "I'll send Tony to get yours in a moment. Kent mentioned a package arrived for you this morning. I'll bring it back with me in a few."

"Thanks, Tom. I'll be here." Brent smiled and knocked on his new cast.

Peaceful quietness settled around the room, enveloping him in its cocoon. Stress had its merits when necessary. Relaxation brought release and renewal. Time to indulge in a huge chunk of it. Closing his eyes, Brent breathed deeply and leaned back. Metal banged against metal, clanging close to him. He cracked open an eye and glanced to his side. His crutches had fallen against his wheelchair. He went back to relaxing and going over his doctor's appointment.

* * * *

After the third pass of the imaging cylinder, Brent opened his eyes. His hands itched. Sweat pooled over his palms. How much longer did he have to lay here? The technician assured him two to three more minutes, and he could sit up.

Glancing sideways, he saw the three doctors talking animatedly. He wished he read lips. Alright, so he hated not knowing and feeling out of control. Bunny pegged him good when she'd accused him of not delegating enough and trusting others to get the job done. He wished she'd been with him. Yet, the overwhelming urge to do this on his own wouldn't leave. Had he made the right decision?

"Mr. Stephens, we've got good news and bad for you." The surgeon smiled. *Oh shit! Breathe, Brent. Breathe,* raced through his psyche. *Remember what the specialist said.*

"Okay, I guess the bad first." Brent shrugged and added, "Can't change what is, right?"

The surgeon moved closer. "No, you can't." He offered his hand and helped Brent sit up. "The chair and cast are necessary for a while longer."

Brent tried muffling the groan threatening to escape. "Sorry," Brent offered.

"No problem. Let me finish, and Dr. Sanders will explain what's next." Brent nodded and gripped the table's edge.

"We want to get you mobile as quickly as possible. The agreement is no surgery is needed."

"Thank you. Should I ask for the good?"

"I'll let my colleagues give you that. Congrats on healing so well! Bye."

No sooner had the surgeon departed than the specialist's pager buzzed. He looked at it and frowned. "I'll be brief. Your tendons need physical therapy. That will wait until your fractures are completely knitted. I'm needed in emergency. Dr. Sanders, I'll be in touch."

Brent's eyes turned to his doctor. What next? How complex was the rest?

Dr. Sanders pushed the wheelchair closer. "Come on. Let's get you down to casting. I'll explain on the way."

Brent slid off the table and hopped on one leg the short distance to the wheelchair. A giddy, nervous energy raced over him at the movement sans his weighted cast. Settling in the chair, he sighed. "Guess that's as good as it gets for a while."

Dr. Sanders's chuckles drew Brent's attention. "Glad I could entertain you."

"Actually," Dr. Sanders began while he pushed Brent through the double doors before them, "there's going to be much more." Brent snapped his head back, trying to focus on Dr. Sanders.

"Better watch where we're going. I'm not a great backseat driver."

Brent grinned at the mirth in Dr. Sanders's tone. "All right."

"As I was saying, there's more coming. Your fractures are healing at a good rate. The surgeon sees no need for pins or surgery. He found no other issues or concerns. As with the specialist, your Achilles tendon not only is sprained but stretched and tight. You need to strengthen it and regain movement."

Brent's hand shot up. "Where's the cast come in?"

"Continued support while the breaks finish healing. About three weeks more is the estimate. Meanwhile, getting you standing more and back to moving around is our next step."

The sign in front of them read "Welcome to Casting". Dr. Sanders gripped Brent's shoulder. "Don't try any fancy footwork on the crutches for a few days. Continue to use the chair some. Increase your time upright and using the crutches to get around. The support boot will help protect the cast and let your ankle take very limited weight bearing."

"You mean I can kiss my chrome buddy good-bye?" Brent chuckled, patting the wheelchair's tires.

"Not quite. Soon, though. Just remember, short forays on the crutches. Stand more. Sit less. Use the boot when standing and with the crutches. Only limited weight on the ankle."

Brent shot the doctor two thumbs up. His smiled widened at the doctor's next words.

"Stop by my office on your way out. I'll have a limited return-to-work release ready for you. And a prescription for low-grade pain meds and at-home exercises to help get you moving easier."

Thirty minutes later, a light gray cast adored his leg from mid-calf down to his arch. Grasping the back of his knee, he lifted his leg off the casting table.

"Mr. Stephens, what are you doing?" His technician grinned as he looked from his leg to her. "The cast is fiberglass. Try moving your leg by itself."

He moved his hand to the table for support as he sat on the edge. Flexing his knee, he rocked his limb back and forth. His first swing rose with enough force to send him flying backwards. He grabbed the table and snorted.

"Easy, Mr. Stephens," the technician offered, adding her laughter to his. "See, nothing like the old one."

"That's for sure. Gotta be careful or I might boot myself in the ass, eh?" He sat upright, enjoying his new range of motion.

"Dr. Sanders wants you to use a knee-high support boot with your crutches. It'll add some weight to your leg at first. Once you're used to the combination, getting around will be easy."

The technician explained how the boot fastened and had Brent stand for modifications. Next came his crutches. His eyes must have glowed because the tech stopped a few feet from him.

"Yeah, I'm savoring those." He pointed to the lightweight aluminum she held. "To stand erect again amongst my peers. Ah, sweetness."

"Too much sitting?" she asked, handing them to him. "Take it slow and easy as you stand. I'll measure you for adjustments."

Five minutes passed, and Brent began to wobble. His uninjured leg throbbed incessantly. He wanted to slump and support his weight on the crutches.

"Try to avoid that unless you want sore armpits and shoulders."

Back in the chair, Brent waited for his escort back to his doctor's office. Closing his eyes, he sighed and grinned. Wiggling his toes felt great. Not that he'd rank it over sex.

Two shrill, short rings interrupted his musings. "Brent Stephens." He glanced at the caller ID display. "Hey, Tony. Right on time. Yes, come on. I'll meet you at the main entrance."

* * * *

Bunny paused, looking at the calendar inside the large storage pantry next to her office. Where had the time flown? Three weeks into November and the holidays were not far off. Rechecking her hash mark totals, she tallied her supply order and added the additional items Ben needed for his holiday pies.

Two car doors slammed outside the open kitchen window. A male voice called out. "Mom, where the hell are you?"

Phillip. Bunny sighed. Would he ever figure out he didn't need to announce his entrance to her and the neighbors? Shaking her head, she smiled. He was home, and that was good. Had he brought someone with him?

Female laughter followed. "Phillip, do you think you could be less vocal and more helpful?"

Bunny's smile grew. Christy had arrived, as well.

Bunny turned down the flame under the pot of egg noodles. Homemade lasagna a la Mom with parmesan garlic butter, French bread, and a tossed salad would feed her hungry family. If Kate wandered in soon, she'd need to set an extra place at the table.

Opening the door, chaos greeted her. Phillip unloaded three suitcases and two boxes. Christy stood nearby, hands on her hips, tapping her foot. Near her sat a small overnight bag and a medium-sized backpack. Her two oldest had arrived home safe and sound. They would grace her with their presence and add to the joy already filling her heart. And multiply the love already there.

"Phillip, for a short stay, I'd say you've over-packed again." Bunny walked up to her son. He grabbed her up in a fierce hug and swung her around.

"Well, you never know what a guy might need." His quick peck on the cheek and wink broadened her smile. Christy moved closer and slid her arm around Bunny's waist.

"Hey, Mom." Christy leaned closer and whispered, "Don't let on. He thinks you need chaperoning with Brent. Really, he's taken a job nearby and needs a temporary place to light."

"Oh?" How would this add to the mix? How long did Phillip plan on staying? And what made him think his mother needed supervision?

"Phillip, what is with all this junk?" Bunny pointed at the growing pile.

His sheepish grin and shrug confirmed Christy's hastily shared whisper.

"You're moving back home?" Bunny folded her arms and glared at him. Damn the boy was just as stubborn and dunderheaded as Derrick. Act first, ask second.

"Come on, Mom. A guy needs a place to lay his head. You never said I couldn't."

"You didn't ask. Phillip, things have changed, and your nonchalant approach to assuming is stopping here and now."

Christy picked up her things and moved toward the door. "Are our rooms ready?"

Bunny spun toward Christy. "Look, both of you. You're welcome to visit and stay for a while. But moving home or showing up unexpectedly is no longer acceptable without prior notice. Phillip, we'll talk about this later. For now, each of you are back in your old rooms."

Phillip turned and looked at his sister. Christy shrugged and followed Bunny inside. Bunny stomped off toward the open door.

Ben greeted them as they sat down in the diner. He sat the pot of coffee and three cups down.

"Coffee?" Bunny poured three cups at Phillip and Christy's silent nods. "Now I am going to speak first, and you two will hear me out."

Phillip creamed his coffee while Christy sweetened hers.

"I know you want what is best for the family. Each of you are grown and on your own. It's time I got a life besides you and your sisters. Kate is fine with it. Why aren't you?"

Phillip looked at Christy and remained silent. Christy sipped her coffee and did not speak.

Bunny counted to ten and continued. "I'm in love with Brent. Now how are you going to handle it? He is due here for dinner soon."

Phillip cleared his throat. "Mom, I don't know what to say. I need a place to light for a while since I got a job over in Anniston. I don't know the guy and certainly am not going to pass judgment until I meet him. You always said someday there might be a new dad for us. I want you to be happy."

Christy tapped her cup with her spoon. Phillip and Bunny turned to her. "I agree with Phillip. I came to meet Brent and spend time with Kate and you. Phillip indicated as much once he told me about getting the new job. We want the best for you and Kate. If Brent is part of that, then we're fine with it."

"Mom," Phillip began, "I don't expect you to remain single or alone. I know Christy doesn't either. But this is still our home, too, and we need to know you are happy and being well treated. We know you can take care of yourself and Kate. Can this guy—Brent—pull his weight and be there for you, too?"

Tears threatened to mist her vision. Warmth enveloped her. Love hadn't passed her by or left her out in the cold. She'd taught her children how to be open to the potential risks and rewards love offered. They'd done her proud. She hoped they approved of Brent.

"There's one more thing you need to know," Bunny stated.

Chapter Fifteen

The loud din of traffic, sirens, and the bell on the diner's front entrance drowned out Bunny's next statement. Noisy walkie-talkie squawks echoed, and a familiar male voice brought a smile to her.

"Excuse me." Bunny stood and moved toward the door. Brent was back. He had a squawk box as they'd jokingly called the walkie-talkies. Why did he? His upbeat tone and positive pitch indicated his improved mood. As she reached the access, her smile faltered. He was still in the chair, with his ankle propped up in front of him. Maybe he'd gotten some good news. She hesitated, waiting for him to clear the entry.

"Tony, I'm at Kater's. Yell if you need me. I'll get back to you in a while otherwise."

Bunny moved forward. She watched Brent deftly maneuver through the access and up the short incline he and Ben had built to accommodate easy admission so he didn't have to yell or ask for help. Grit and determination etched across his face the last few feet to her. He rolled up alongside her and swiftly grabbed her hand.

Bunny stumbled frontward. Putting her hand out, she tried to halt her fall and yelped. "Brent!"

"Come here, sweetness." His low, husky tone made her blush. His eyes sparkled as he saw her face. "Oh, so the lady is embarrassed?"

Bunny swallowed hard. He wasn't helping. She nodded toward Phillip and Christy. "We've got company."

"Oops. Sorry." Brent's chaste peck on her cheek raised her temperature and not in a way she welcomed.

Leaning closer, she whispered. "Phillip and Christy arrived this afternoon. I hope their first impression is a good one."

Brent laughed. "Darling, they're grown. Surely they understand what happens between the sexes."

"Umm, yes. But we don't need to show them how."

Brent released her hand and wheeled forward.

"Phillip. Christy. I'm Brent." He offered his hand to Phillip. "Pleasure to meet you."

Christy nudged Phillip. Bunny grinned. There were few times either was at a loss for words.

"Hey, Ben," Brent called out. "Can I get some coffee, too?"

"Coming up, Mr. Brent."

Bunny took her seat and entwined her fingers with Brent's, beneath the table.

"Your coffee." Ben set a large carryout cup before Brent.

"How did you know?" Brent searched Ben's face.

"Tony and the squawk box." Ben grinned and raised his apron, pointing to a smaller version hanging from his waist. "Ever since you've been staying here, Tony and I coordinated to make sure you knew what was going on or if you were needed."

Brent squeezed Bunny's hand. "Thanks, Ben. I'm a bit past motherhening. I appreciate the concern."

"No problem, Mr. Brent. You're one of the family. We take care of each other. Right, Mr. Phillip, Ms. Christy?"

Bunny's subdued snicker caught Brent's attention. Her slight nod to Christy and Phillip drew his gaze. Brent bit his lip to keep from laughing.

Christy sat upright, toying with her spoon, her eyes on Brent. Phillip ducked his head and averted Ben's stern look. Bunny's whisper made Brent cough as more laughter threatened. "Ben's sergeant stare should be in every mother's arsenal."

Brent smiled and winked at Bunny. Her last remark confirmed a lot. Ben was a valuable ally to have. His and Ben's late night talks revealed what an integral asset Ben was to Bunny and her children. He'd been the doting uncle and surrogate father when needed.

"Ben, is there any of your rum cake to be had? I think we could all use a slice to hold us till dinner," Brent asked. He turned to Christy. "I didn't get a chance to greet you when you brought Kate home last time."

"I wish I hadn't rushed off, and we'd gotten a chance to talk." Christy grinned at him.

Low volume discourse crackled out the walkie-talkie sitting atop the table.

"Chief, Tony here. Tom has that box you were asking for."

"Okay. Put it in the safe for now. Thanks, Tony." Brent turned off the volume.

Phillip raised his head. Brent inhaled sharply. It was Derrick's face that looked back at him. His father's eyes. They gave him the once over. Brent cleared his throat. "What do you want to know?"

The creaking of the kitchen door swinging open cut the silence filling the room. Ben's snort and clatter of plates followed. The clanging of silverware on the table made them laugh.

Christy spoke first. "How do you feel about Mom?"

"I care deeply for her." Brent faced Phillip. "Your turn."

"What do you want from her?" He watched Phillip nervously rub his lips together.

"I want her to be my significant other. The person I turn to for companionship, caring, concern, and whatever else she's willing to give."

Phillip started to say more. Instead, he grunted and narrowed his eyes at Christy.

Bunny tapped the table. "Brent and I are a couple. We're exploring and learning together. Some things we aren't going to answer. So choose your questions wisely."

Brent burst out laughing. "I concur with her. I'll give you the brief, and then I have to get back to work."

"Work?" Bunny asked.

"Work," Brent answered, short and to the point. "I'll explain later." He rolled back and closer to Phillip and Christy. He placed his hands on the table.

"I'm a firefighter like your dad was. I'm commander of the station next door and the fire chief. We've known each other for a while and began dating a few months ago."

"So you know about Dad and Grandma?" Christy asked.

"Yes, and Bunny knows things from my past. Like she said, we're learning and exploring together."

Brent put his hand on Phillip's shoulder. "You haven't said much. I'm not looking to take your dad's place."

"Thanks. It's different and going to take getting used to. Ben's been as close to a dad as we've had for a long time." Phillip blinked several times as though he attempted to hold back tears. Brent patted his shoulder.

"Sometimes change brings healing or resurfaces what we thought was over. Maybe you and I can talk more when I'm off duty."

"Yeah, I'd like that." Phillip offered Brent his hand. "I didn't shake earlier. How about now?"

Brent firmly shook Phillip's hand. "No problem. I want you both to know I love your mother. I want the best for all of us."

Brent glanced at his watch. "Ben, thanks for the coffee. Keep a plate warm for me, please. I'll squawk box ya when I'm ready."

Ben smiled and nodded.

The jangle of bells sounded. Kate entered and hurried over to Brent.

"Brent, we did it! Thank you!" She threw her arms around his neck and kissed his cheek. Her smile grew as she faced Bunny, seeing her brother and sister. "You're here! Great!"

"What happened?" Bunny asked. What had Brent been coaching Kate on?

"Our debate squad won regionals. We're going to state finals."
Kate's enthusiasm was catchy. Brent's smile echoed hers.

"That's great, Kate!" He raised his hand and high-fived her.

"Will you help me practice and prepare for finals?"

"Sure, hon. Get all your stuff together like last time, and we'll
strategize. Come over later, and we'll talk. I'm manning dispatch."

Brent hugged Kate. "See you about eight."

Bunny stood, still keeping her brood in focus. So far so good. No
issues she could pinpoint. She'd wait until Brent left to find out.

Bunny returned and found the three sitting and talking together
after seeing Brent off. "Kate, are you staying for dinner?'

"Yes, I've got two exams to study for. I'm glad Phillip is here. He
can help me with my civics project. He draws better than I do."

Bunny looked to Phillip. His grin and shrug eased her. "Okay,
dinner is almost ready. Set an extra place, please."

Phillip began following Kate. "Phillip, one moment. I need to ask
you something."

* * * *

Brent turned down the volume to prevent further echoes in the
radio room. Central dispatch two counties over was replacing their
phone banks in twelve-hour shift slots. Tomorrow Jameston would be
back online. For now, they were on their own.

A small, black velvet box sat before him. Its ornate pink markings
warmed him. Childhood memories flashed to the surface. Rumpled
paper lay next to it, Randy's strong handwriting upon it.

Brent,

*Good luck. Tara grinned and clapped when I told her. Mom cried
as she smiled, and Grandma nodded and began asking questions.
Mom's sure this is the one. Marta didn't rate this high.*

Call soon! Please! Unless you want a horde of family members descending upon you. You know how stubborn and impatient some of them can be.

Love,

Randy

Brent pushed Randy's note aside and pulled the box to him. His late father's admonishment came to mind as he touched it.

Never take lightly asking someone to share your life. It takes work and commitment. Neither is ever finished. It's an ongoing project, a work in progress. I hope you find someone worthy of the task.

Brent smiled. "I have, Dad. Thanks for the advice." He shuddered as though a chill enveloped him. Had a voice just whispered, *"You're welcome, son"*? Brent spun around and found himself alone. Shrugging, he opened the box.

A solitaire two-carat diamond winked at him. Its delicate, filigree-etched silver band with Celtic symbols cradled it. Memories flooded him as he held it, his mother lovingly cleaning and cherishing the ring over the years. He remembered in particular her tears as she removed it two years after Dad's death. She said the time had come to move on and let the next generation of Stephenses build happy times with it.

The moment was now. He hoped Bunny agreed. Whether they went slow or proceeded with small steps, he didn't care. He'd waited a long time to find the one, and he'd found her. Was everyone onboard?

Sounds of approaching footsteps echoed across the empty truck bay. The ambulance crew was on a call. And the fire engine sat outside ready to roll if needed. Brent looked at the digital time stamp clock. Ten p.m. Had Kate forgotten something? She appeared to have all her stuff when she departed an hour earlier. Picking up the remote dispatch radio and dropping the ring in his front shirt pocket, he wheeled to the door. A lovely vision greeted him.

Bunny, carrying food and a thermos, moved toward him. Spices and hefty aromas teased his nose and taste buds. She'd hinted at dinner's ingredients when she'd walked him out. He'd asked Kate to have her mother bring over his plate since he'd told Ben no a couple hours prior.

"Woman, you look good enough to eat," he teased, moving closer. "Not to mention, you smell great, too. What is that cologne you're wearing?"

Bunny shook her head and smiled. "You know, there's a saying about the way to a man's heart is through his stomach. I wonder why someone hasn't retailed food aroma perfumes." Their combined laughter bounced off the bay's walls.

"Come on in the radio room." Brent turned toward the door he'd just come through. "There's less noise in there, and we can be heard without recourse or worrying about others in or out of the station knowing our discussion."

* * * *

Bunny pulled up the extra chair to the right of the desk and sat. Brent's hearty appetite hadn't waned, and she took pleasure in watching him enjoy eating. It continued to amaze her how much he could eat and not gain weight. She knew she looked forward to his return to mobility and their mutual jogs.

"I'm glad you enjoy my cooking. Phillip and Christy ate two plates full and asked for the leftovers to be frozen to take with them. I am wondering at Phillip's earlier remark, if he'll be taking his with him."

"Why? What did he say?" Brent's questioning look and silence relieved her some. His willingness to hear her out and not jump in hadn't been easy for them to work out. She knew he wanted to know and help. Still, he kept on eating and let her decide when to speak. Another reason she'd fallen in love with him.

"Seems he's taken a job in Anniston and needs to find a place. But the job starts next week, and he's not found a place yet. He mentioned staying with me."

"Oh?" Brent asked in between bites. "Isn't that awkward given current conditions?"

"It might have been if things hadn't changed." She munched on a breadstick, waiting to see if Brent would offer his opinion or continue questioning her.

Wiping his mouth, he laid down his fork and pointed at the small container near the thermos. "What's in there?"

Though she was a bit irked at his deliberate change of subject, she was pleased he hadn't jumped in to save her or work some male-inspired miracle. She opened the thermos and poured.

"Ben made sure you and I got the last two pieces of his pumpkin rum cake topped with Irish coffee flavored icing. I added decaffeinated English breakfast tea to the menu, figuring you might be coffeed out."

"Oh, woman, you know me too well." Brent grinned and winked. "My stomach and taste buds thank you."

"You're welcome. I wish Phillip had asked about moving in or staying with me." She sighed and let go a deep, pent-up breath.

"Are you asking me for my thoughts? Or venting?" Brent cut the cake in half and moved her portion towards her. "You seem to have a lot on your mind."

"Both. This affects you, too. You've been staying in his room. And it feels good to have someone to share with and talk it out."

"Well, he's your son, and I know how I would feel if someone I just met told me I couldn't stay in my family home. On the other hand, it does complicate things and make changes imminent. What did you decide or come up with as solutions?"

What a gem. Brent hadn't tried to fix the issue or bowl her over with the rightness of his thoughts or conclusions. He was actively partnering with her to resolve things. Yes, he was a keeper in more ways than she realized before. She hoped he liked what she'd decided.

"Phillip moved into the room at the top of stairs since his furniture is in storage until he gets his own place. He has a couple of applications in near his new job." Bunny hesitated before going on. The next part really came first, but apprehension and uncertainty ruled her decision to state it last.

Brent sat back, cradling his cup of tea and watched her attentively. Damn, at times, his being able to read her unnerved her more than it helped. Yet, his uncanny knack for knowing that something bothered her or she needed time to think things through aided the strength of her verdict. She was going to risk being in a relationship with him and allow herself to be vulnerable again. Licking her lips, she knew it was time.

"I moved your stuff in with me. I made the choice before they arrived. Did you and Tom discuss anything besides work?"

* * * *

Brent nodded slightly. How fast had she decided to shift into roomies mode? What were her motives after several weeks of needing to keep Kate from knowing about them? While he wanted to believe her choices came from her heart, his conscience nagged him, and his gut didn't quite settle.

"Penny for your thoughts." Bunny twisted her cup and picked at her cake.

"Sweetie, I'm glad you made your own choices. I'm fine with Phillip's decision to take one of the bed and breakfast rooms. He could've stayed in his old room, too. I'm uncertain as to why you moved my things before he arrived. Care to share the reason."

Why was she fidgeting with her cup and crumbling her cake? Did the motive really matter? *Yeah*, his pain in the ass conscience yelled along with his flip-flopping stomach. It was better to know than to guess and be unsure. Where had he heard those words before? Ah yes, Marta, several months after their bitter divorce. Ask and seek to know, but reserve judgments when its due and hold no grudges were her parting words to him her last day alive. So the question remained as to why, and her reasons. Encouraging her to share would benefit them both.

"Whatever your answers, I want to know. Clear communication between us is vital to our relationship growing and nurturing what we already have. I may not like them, but they're important to you and so I need to hear you out."

"I've got a question I need answered."

It was the first she'd looked up in over five minutes. He'd respond as best he could. "Sure. What is it?"

Chapter Sixteen

"Work," she stated without pause or preamble. "What is going on? You've not talked about your doctor's appointment or the results. You mentioned work and told me nothing."

Ah shit, his turn to fidget and squirm. He wanted to wait until he knew what was going on in her heart and head before he spilled his news. That wasn't going to happen easily. Deliberately ignoring the issue wouldn't help nor could it ease a damn thing. He was between a rock and a huge freakin' boulder. All right, he'd try the give and take approach. Ask a few questions, share some answers, and see where it got them.

"If it were simple, I'd explain it all. Suffice to say, I am with my wheels for a while longer. Got a new cast. What about my earlier questions?"

Bunny glanced at his ankle. She leaned forward to get a better view. "Hey, your leg is down." Rocking back in her chair, she folded her arms across her chest and glared. "When were you going to tell me about this?"

Brent sat his cup on the desk and glowered. "Are we at an impasse here? You want to know more and so do I. So how about we each take a turn and update the other?"

Bunny nodded her consent and relaxed her posture. "I decided to move your things for two reasons. One, Phillip has a hard time sharing his space. As the only male in the family until now, he's valued his personal area. I figured it would be easier to say we were sharing my room than to clarify details that are none of their business."

"Okay, but what about Kate knowing about us and our sleeping together? Isn't it two-faced to tell the others and not her?" Brent moved their cups and containers to the side and reached for her hand. "What is reason two?"

Her impish grin caught him by surprise. Tendrils of warmth inched down his arm and chest each time his heart thrummed. What was she about to expose? Last time that grin happened, he was tied up and chocolate-covered. Lord, he hoped her mind hadn't decided a trip down memory lane was in order.

She stood and moved very close to him. Her fingers threaded in his hair and massaged his scalp. Much more and he'd have a hard-on that refused to behave. Yet, he missed and craved her touch. A few minutes couldn't hurt. Could it?

As quickly as she'd started, she stopped and grabbed the arm of the wheelchair. Great. How did he tell her no and not ruin their discussion? "I think we'd better—"

She spun him around, stopping him as he faced her. A deep smile spread to her eyes and seemed to make them glow. Not taking his gaze off her, he watched her every move. Something was percolating in that naughty mind of hers. He looked down to catch his breath and ask her what was going on.

Too late, she sat straddling his lap. Her mons hovered over his inquiring cock. Last thing he needed was cum stains on his uniform pants. "Sweetie, this would be fun if I wasn't on duty."

"Shh," she admonished and put her fingers over his lips. "I have something to say."

Brent nodded and kissed her fingers. Her silent *oh* nudged his cock to full alert. So much for turning the heat down. Her wink and airborne kiss didn't help either. *Listen*, he repeated like a well rehearsed mantra. He hoped she revealed her second reason soon.

"I..." She kissed his cheek and nibbled his jaw line. His internal thermostat hit medium done. Her inner vixen was in control. *Cool down* became his new phrase.

"Love…" Her tongue slipped up and around his ear lobe. *God, the wanton woman was loose again.* Not that he was complaining.

"You." The last word fell huskily in his ear as her teeth worried his ear lobe and sent him into steaming.

Brent pulled back panting and framed her face with his hands. Control—he needed to get it and regain composure. Had she just said what he thought she had? His brain rebuffed any change from horniness. At least his blasted libido did. Two deep breaths and three short breaths. Count to five. The exercises his therapist recommended to help with his stress only did so much. His heat level cooled some, and he eased Bunny sideways on his lap.

"You love me? Did I hear you correctly?"

Her deep smile and rapid nod confirmed he heard her right. Wrapping his arms around her waist, he hugged her tightly and rested his chin atop her head, closing his eyes. His silent prayer winged heavenward, and he added a special thank you to his dad and late ex.

Bunny snuggled against him and draped her arm loosely around his shoulders. Neither spoke for a moment or two until the dispatch radio hummed, and the alarm jarred them both back into the now.

"Damn," he growled. "Hang on. We need to talk more. I have to take care of this first."

"Jameston here. Where is the fire located? And how many more do you need for assistance?" Brent pulled a pad to him and began scribbling. He tore off the top sheet and passed it to Bunny. She hastily read it and nodded. He hoped one engine was enough. He couldn't spare both.

* * * *

"Kent!" Bunny yelled as she raced up the stairs to the upper level housing the staff's quarters. "Brent needs you and the six most rested men stat. There's a fire in Jackson needing backup."

Kent met her at the top of the stairs, pulling on his shirt. "Ms. Bunny, we're on our way."

* * * *

Ten minutes later, quiet ruled the station again. Brent sat with Bunny nestled on his lap, listening to her happily hum. He wished the moment didn't have to end. Alas, it did. She needed answers to her questions.

"Love, we need to talk. It'll be easier without you on my lap."

She rose and pulled the other chair closer. "I'm listening." She took his hands in hers.

Brent swallowed hard. He wanted to accept her declaration of love without preamble or clarification. His heart and gut said no. If he did nothing else, he needed to tell her what the doctor had said.

"I'm going to lay it out straight. I know no other way to prevent misunderstandings." He paused, wanting to ensure she heard him and didn't take him to task over it later.

"Go ahead." She dropped his hands and sat back.

"I don't need surgery, though I messed up my Achilles tendon pretty bad. The compound fractures are healing nicely. Still I have miles to go before I am fully mobile and without this." He knocked on his cast.

"I'm glad you're not facing surgery. That must be a huge load off your mind. Where does work fit into this?"

He hated answering a question with a question. Her response charted his wording.

"Why do you love me?" There, he said it, and the boulder was off his chest. But, now the damn thing was on the desk between them. Or was it?

Bunny toyed with his fingers and didn't say a word. Had he blown it? His heart took two extra beats each time she touched him. He wanted to coax her into saying something. That wasn't fair if she wasn't ready to speak. How much longer did he have to wait? He was running low on patience and virtue.

"I love you because you're different. You're not Derrick or any of the other men I've dated or made friends with over the years. There's a uniqueness that draws me and compels me to love you. I think I'm guilty of seeing or judging most men through my Derrick-coated lenses."

Talk about a mouth full, but he'd asked for it. He wasn't Derrick in many regards, and her ability to see him for himself was good. He'd never be anyone else. Still, there were similarities mostly due to work. His turn to reveal more.

"There is an area where he and I are the same. Have you given that any consideration?"

Her two short, shallow breaths told him she hadn't thought much about how his job affected her. She hadn't come to terms with him returning to work. He'd opened the complex issue, so he'd help her along.

"Can you love me even if I return to firefighting? Does your love encompass the possibility that I, too, might die in the line of duty?"

"Are you trying to scare me?" Bunny's agitated voice almost screeched like fingernails roughing down a chalkboard. A bone of contention, maybe a sore spot. They had to work it out and come to a decision. It might not be clear-cut. She needed to accept him completely, and he needed to know she really saw him. No more distorted images that left her hurt and distrustful again.

"No, I'm not. You asked about work. This is who I am and what I love doing. I'm a firefighter. I save lives and take risks. Often high risks come with the position. Are you ready to accept that? Take that chance with me?"

Bunny's heavy sigh and pent-up tears crashed over his flopping heart. Had they reached a point of no return? How far had she come? How much was he willing to compromise?

"Brent, I don't know. I'll be honest with you in that it frightens me. Derrick's motivations and drives aren't yours, and yet, I can't shake this feeling that fuels my uncertainty. I want you in my life and part of it." She stood and dropped his hands. She reached for the dishes.

His hand stopped her. "Are you saying no?"

"No, I'm saying I'm still nervous about you being a fireman. I need to think and mull over the possibilities and such. Deal with my demons and slay my inner dragons or placate them. Either way, I need some time on this."

"Maybe it's better I stay at the station tonight. Give you some time alone," he offered, knowing his heart screamed *no* with each beat.

"That's not necessary. I've grown accustomed to your snores and being beside me. I don't want you to leave. I just need time to adjust. We'll talk when you get home. Ben is taking the early shift along with Phillip and Christy."

Bunny's retreat out the door sent shivers down his back and across his shoulders. A heavy, dark feeling invaded his heart. Had he pushed her too far?

Chapter Seventeen

Bunny's eyes flew open. What was that noise? "Brent, did you hear that?"

Her hand reached out for him. Nothing. Sitting up, she flicked on the bedside lamp and squinted at clock. One a.m. Where was he? As her vision cleared, she turned toward his side of the bed.

It was as she'd left it before going to sleep. The blankets were folded back, and his pillows slightly angled. No indentation showed where his head would have touched them. Why?

She remembered sitting with her knees drawn up, waiting for him. Two pens and several sheets of paper sat where she'd left them in the middle of the bed. A few tearstains caught her eye. His hard questions deserved answers, and she was ready to share them. Her mind had moved so fast that writing down her ideas and random thoughts allowed her to capture her true feelings. Now she understood why he'd asked and probed. She couldn't share if he wasn't here.

A similar noise startled her. Shoving her feet into her slippers and pulling on her bathrobe, she called out. "Brent, is that you?" No answer.

She ventured into the hall, turning on lights as she went. She opened the door to Phillip's old room, illuminating the empty bed. A rustling of paper and footsteps drew her into the hallway. Paper crunched again. This time it came from down the hall. She crept toward the sound. Low voices came from another direction. Burglars?

Once her night vision kicked in, she saw the small beam of light coming from under Kate's door. She must still be up studying or had fallen asleep with books and papers on her bed.

Voices sounded again, somewhere near the kitchen. She couldn't quite make out the words. Tiptoeing to the kitchen door, she flicked on the overhead lights and yelled out, "Someone call 911!"

"Mom?" three voices called out. "Where are you?"

"In the kitchen," she answered.

Moving forward, she found the source of the noise. Ben's squawk box hung charging next to the phone. He must have forgotten to turn it off when he left.

Lights flooded the dining room, and Phillip stood beside her. "You okay?"

"Yes, I think so." She turned to find Christy and Kate filling the door behind her. Where was Brent?

Her heart refused to stop its pitter-pattering race, and adrenaline surged through her, pumping into her already nervous state. "Phillip, have you seen Brent?" She faced the open serving window, wondering if he sat out of harm's way waiting for the ruckus to stop.

Bunny glanced around the dining room. Brent's empty wheelchair sat next to the table near the front door. His usual coffee mug bearing his name set on the table next to several sheets of paper along with a dispatch radio. It crackled and hummed as calls sounded.

Phillip stepped closer. "We talked some around midnight when he came in. He mentioned that putting them back on central dispatch ran later than expected. He said he was turning in as soon as Tom or Tony picked up the radio."

Moving toward the door, she looked toward the station. Lights and activity showed through the open bay doors. Phillip reached her side. "Mom, want me to come with you?"

"No." Bunny picked up the papers from the table and leafed through them. Duty rosters, payroll vouchers, and acquisition forms greeted her until she reached the bottom sheet. She scanned its contents.

Doctor's orders for continued physical therapy confirmed their earlier discussion. She read on aloud. "Limited mobility on crutches.

No more than fifteen to twenty minutes intervals until—" Muffled crackling followed by garbled speech came from Brent's radio.

"Is that Brent?" Phillip reached for the radio. Bunny stayed his hand.

"Yes. I'll check on him." She squeezed Phillip's hand. "Thanks for offering to go with me. This is between Brent and me." She started toward the door.

"Mom?" Christie's call stopped her. Bunny turned.

They stood together, Phillip's arms around Christie and Kate. Their concerned looks tugged at her conscience. This didn't just affect her. It mattered to all of them.

"What, Christie?" She motioned them forward. Kate reached Bunny first and hugged her tightly. Phillip came next and finally Christie.

Christie stepped back, glancing from her brother to her sister. "We care, too."

Bunny smiled and nodded.

"I know." Her voice cracked and failed her as she tried to continue. She cleared her throat and went on. "Give me fifteen minutes before you descend upon us, okay?"

Their silent nods encouraged her.

Bunny dashed out the front door. Its unlocked state didn't faze her. She jumped down the few steps between her and the sidewalk. One thing mattered. Brent. Was he all right?

Holding her side, she rushed in through the open bay door. Her gaze darted over the people closest to her. She moved quickly toward Amy who stood farther back near Brent's office. "Amy, have you—"

Amy moved aside and behind her, he stood. *Stood?* Bunny's brain repeated the word like a broken record. She stumbled forward, her hands outstretched. "Brent?"

"Excuse me, Amy." He moved past her. He crutched forward, stopping every few strides.

Bunny shook her head and stepped closer. "Why didn't you tell me?"

"Pride and a stubborn heart. Woman, you mean the world to me. I'm sorry—"

She clapped her hand over his mouth. "For once, shut up and listen." His narrowed eyes prompted her addition. "Please."

At his nod, she continued. "I guess we're both mulish and prideful. I owe you a thank you. If you hadn't asked the hard questions, the insulation around my heart would still be there. I love you no matter what."

Brent dropped one of his crutches and wrapped his arm around her waist. "Are you sure?" he asked resting his forehead on hers. "I'm willing—"

She cut him short again. This time with her lips. She poured her heart and soul into her kiss. Did he get it?

"Wow!" someone called out, followed by, "Whoa, Mom and Brent! Get a room!"

His lips moved over hers, deepening their kiss. Her eyes closed, and she opened to his seeking tongue. Soon their mouths mimicked what their bodies craved. Wait. Had he said something? Stated words as they kissed?

"In my pocket." His muffled words reached her ears.

"Huh?" Bunny asked, pulling back and ending the kiss.

"Look in my pocket. I can't reach, or I'll fall." His eyes begged her to do what he asked. The sparkle and joy lighting them urged her to do as he requested.

She patted the one closest to her. A male nipple peaked under her rough touch. "I, uh, I don't think that is what you wanted. Was it?" she whispered, glancing sideways, suddenly aware of the crowd surrounding them. Several of his staff and her children intently watched them.

Throwing back his head, Brent laughed. Deep belly laughs rolled out. "Not at the moment. I'll take a rain check, if you don't mind."

"Chief!" Amy chided. "That's my best friend."

"Oh stop being jealous," Bunny teased. "Now where were we?"

"My pocket. The upper ones for now." Brent winked and grinned at her. "The left one might yield a treasure."

Bunny dragged her fingers up Brent's shirt and outlined his pocket. "Ouch! What is that?"

"Take a look and find out."

Reaching inside, she clasped the round object. Her mouth gaped as she withdrew the item.

"Yes," Brent began, "it's what you think it is. Will you spend the rest of your life with me?"

Bunny choked back the tears threatening to fill her eyes and rush down her cheeks. She nodded and buried her face in the front of his shirt.

"Woman, now you're at a loss for words?"

She moved sideways and thrust out her hand, taking the ring and placing on her finger as she yelled out her answer.

"Yes! I'll marry you and spend the rest of my life with you."

Cheers and rancorous yells amongst applause broke out as her children, best friend, and Brent's crew drew closer.

Epilogue

Seven Months Later

"Parents, teachers, and students, I give you Jameston High School's Class of 2009 Valedictorian, Kate Kater."

Brent applauded loudly along with the rest of his new family and the families of the graduating seniors. Beside him sat Bunny with her slightly rounded stomach beginning to show. Their five month anniversary had just passed. Twins, possibly triplets, five months hence still made him weak in the knees. A welcomed and wanted surprise neither had anticipated this soon. Two seats over, Phillip and his fiancée Melissa sat holding hands. Their wedding three weeks hence caught everyone off guard. Tomorrow, celebrations would fill Kater's—Kate's graduation party and a family reunion. Several generations of Stephenses would be visiting. His mother and grandmother couldn't stop talking about the new grandbabies on the way.

Christy smiled at Brent and winked. He laughed quietly, remembering her fierce welcome hug once they'd sorted out her concerns and fears. Even Phillip had come around after a while. Along with Kate, they called him Dad, not wanting their siblings to be to know or feel any less part of the family.

How full and enriched his life had become in such a short time. He'd been warned about red-hot embers and their intensity. He didn't care or want to change the experience or the results. He'd walked through his ring of fire, come out the other side whole, and healed. Bunny squeezed his hand and smiled.

Yes, together and partnered, both knew a lifetime of love and joy awaited them.

THE END

solaragordon.wordpress.com

ABOUT THE AUTHOR

Solara loves and lives with her partner of 12 years in the Metro DC area. What started out as a bi-coastal romance soon settled on one coast.

A vivid imagination keeps her busy creating her next fascinating romance. She enjoys creating unique characters and watching their journeys unfold. "Love freely given multiplies and will return endlessly" is a key aspect of her stories. Add in alternative lifestyles and her love for the paranormal, and the uncommon becomes the norm in many of her stories.

Her day job in the financial services industry pays the bills while she pens her erotic tales.

Siren Publishing, Inc.
www.SirenPublishing.com

LaVergne, TN USA
07 October 2010
199970LV00004B/51/P